D0049152

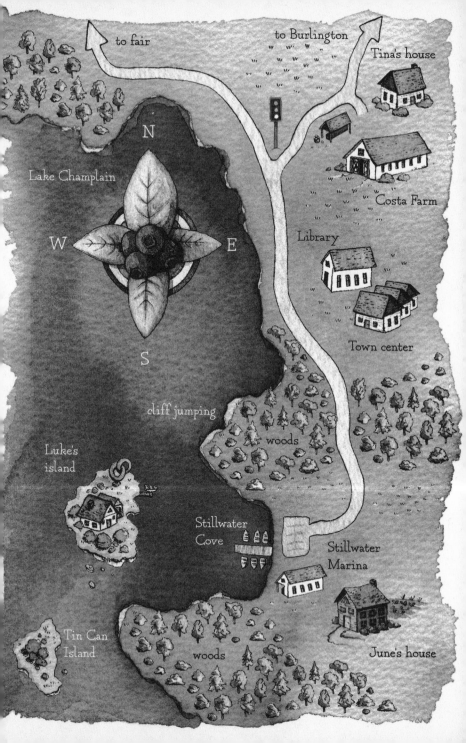

To Hewson, Maggie, Sarah, and Indira,
my first readers. And Breauna, who had to face
grown-up bullies.

Houghton Mifflin Books for Children is an imprint of Houghton Mifflin Harcourt
Publishing Company.

www.hmhbooks.com

The text of this book is set in Fournier MT Std.
The map is pen and inkwash.

Library of Congress Cataloging-in-Publication Data
Gennari, Jennifer.
My mixed-up berry blue summer / by Jennifer Gennari.
p. cm.
Summary: Twelve-year-old June Farrell spends the summer at her Vermont
home getting used to the woman her mother is planning to marry and practicing
her pie-baking skills, as she hopes to win the blue ribbon at the fair.

ISBN 978-0-547-57739-5

[1. Lesbians—Fiction. 2. Prejudices—Fiction. 3. Pies—Fiction. 4. Mothers and
daughters—Fiction. 5. Vermont—Fiction.] I. Title.
PZ7.G29174MY 2012
[Fic]—dc23
2011012240

Manufactured in the United States
DOC 10 9 8 7 6 5 4 3 2 1
4500348247

My Mixed-Up
BERRY BLUE
SUMMER

by
JENNIFER
GENNARI

Houghton Mifflin Books for Children
HOUGHTON MIFFLIN HARCOURT
Boston   New York   2012

UNLIKE SOME PEOPLE, Lake Champlain was a friend I could count on. I knew her every mood—sometimes she was flat like a cookie sheet, and other times she was whipped up like meringue on a butterscotch pie.

That was the way I felt, too. Ever since Eva had moved in with Mom and me last month, I was as changeable as the lake.

I looked out my bedroom window. The lights were already on at Stillwater Marina; Mom was probably boxing pies and wrapping cookies, getting ready for the customers who would tie up at the dock and come into our shop. I'd be there to help her soon. Or maybe I'd swim first. The lake, rolling steadily to shore, was as dark and inviting as rubbed blueberries.

My mouth watered, thinking about blueberry season and tasting the sweet zing of the first berry. What I

needed, though, were champion berries, the kind growing wild on the cliffs around the lake. I was going to make
my best pie ever and enter it into the Champlain Valley
Fair. I could see the newspaper headline already: "Wild
Berry Pie by June Farrell, 12, Astonishes Judges."

The trick to great pies — and I should know — is fruit
combinations. Everybody does strawberry-rhubarb. To
stand out from the crowd, you have to do something
offbeat, like apple-blackberry or strawberry-peach-
pineapple or blueberry-pear. And you need the best in-
gredients, of course — no store-bought blueberries or
hothouse strawberries.

I shrugged out of my PJs and pulled on my bathing
suit. Luke would know where to find wild blueberries.
I stood on my bed and grabbed the large flashlight sus-
pended by fishing line from my curtain rod and covered it
with a green cellophane lens, pointing it west toward the
island just a softball field away from our shore. I trained
my binoculars on Luke's house on the tip of the island and
zoomed in on his window.

He was up — his green light shining back at me. We
had been using the color lenses left over from a school
play for about four years, since we were eight: green — I
can play; yellow — I can't; red — trouble. I wish I could
claim it as my idea. Luke says, when you don't have a
phone, you learn to improvise.

I shifted my gaze to the dock and spotted Luke. His shaggy black hair was in his eyes, his hands carrying oars to the rowboat at the end of his dock. I couldn't wait to hear his plan for the day.

I yanked my Stillwater Marina T-shirt over my bathing suit and pulled my brown hair into a ponytail. I didn't bother looking in the mirror: I was the same June, never mind the changes other people saw. I clambered down from my loft to the kitchen.

"Good morning, June." Eva moved her plate over. "I was just finishing up."

"That's OK." I grabbed a bowl and the Cheerios and sat at the other end of the table. I still couldn't get used to her being here.

In between us was a bowl of sliced strawberries, courtesy of Mom, I was sure. I took a handful for my Cheerios. Strawberry-blueberry-cherry? I wanted the strangest fruit mixture for my pie.

Eva brushed a crumb from her shirt. I could have told her everything was in its place, from her cropped blond hair to her nametag neatly pinned on the right: EVA LEWIS, MD. I balanced the comics upright on the cereal box, hoping she'd get the message.

"OJ?" she asked.

I shook my head and remained behind the box.

She turned to the newspaper, rustling the pages.

"Look at this headline," she said, pointing to "Grassroots Organization Backs Candidates to Repeal Civil Union Law." "Has everyone gone crazy?"

I was sick of hearing about civil unions and gay rights. "Mom says not to worry."

"That's MJ for you." Eva folded the paper on the table. "By the way, a package arrived that has to be unpacked —on top of wrapping all those cookies you two made last night."

"I know what needs to be done." I picked up my bowl and put it down hard in the sink. As if Eva knew anything about the marina shop. She hated boats. I knew how long mooring line was, what kind of oil motorboats needed, and what size cleats were best for main sheets. Mom and I knew how much bread to make for sandwiches and batter for giant batches of peanut butter and chocolate chip cookies.

Eva put her dish in the dishwasher. "MJ asked me to remind you."

"I didn't forget."

"Of course, I'm sorry," she said, glancing at a little milk pooled on the table. I could tell she couldn't wait to clean it up. I'd leave it for her; my eyes were on the lake.

"Luke's here." I banged through the door and down to the dock.

I grabbed the line he tossed my way.

"Hey, June." Luke was dressed like me in a faded

T-shirt and ready to swim. He climbed out of his boat. "Your mom need help?"

"As usual." I tied a quick hitch around the pier cleat.

"When we're done, I've got a new place to show you," he said.

"With blueberries?"

"Yup."

Luke and I turned toward the shop. His strides were longer—he was a head taller than me—but I kept up.

"Does Joe need you to hold a piece of sculpture or anything today?"

"He's still sleeping—he was up late blowtorching."

"Eva's still in the kitchen."

He looked at me sideways. "Fireworks, already?"

I snorted. "She's just so perfect."

"Like me?" He pulled at his faded shirt and made a face.

I laughed. "Yeah, right!" That was one of the things that made Luke so likeable—he didn't care what other people thought. Maybe living on an island was so offbeat, you just had to give up on fitting in.

●　●　●

LUKE AND I found Mom slouched over a book behind the counter, her Stillwater Marina cap pulled low. At the sound of the door, she pushed her cap back and smiled at us.

"There you are," Mom said, turning down a page as she closed her book. "Help me wrap plastic around these cookies — two to a package. Luke, you put the price tag on."

"Anything you say, MJ," Luke said, and stuck a $1.95 sticker on his nose.

I grinned. That's another reason why I like Luke.

"Did you have breakfast with Eva?" she asked me.

"The strawberries you left were perfect," I said. "Made me imagine the perfect pie."

"How about blueberry-pineapple?" Mom said.

I paused to consider the combination, but I shook my head. "I can't get fresh pineapple," I said. "It's gotta be something really good, really surprising."

"Well, corn's coming up soon — why not corn-berry pie?" Luke said. "Or zucchini-apple! Is that weird enough?"

"You're the weird one around here," I said. The plastic wrap stuck together as I stacked two cookies on top. I picked at it to untangle it. I was the strange one, really, living with Mom and Eva. The thought of my unknowable father came to me, again. Was he like Tina's dad, driving a tractor and planting crops, or like Joe, Luke's dad, welding together sculptures he dreamed up in his mind? What I wanted was a dad, not another mother. Instead, I got Eva, all fussy and difficult. I pulled the plastic clumsily around the cookies and stuck a price tag on the bundle. It looked lousy.

Luke was clicking out price tags from the labeling gun, lining them up along the counter.

"Slow down," Mom said. "That's all we need."

"Can we go then?" Luke asked.

She gathered up the wrapped cookies and arranged them in the basket. "OK, but June, please come back for lunch."

The marina door banged shut as we raced out.

"The new spot is up by the old camp," Luke said.

We crossed the road to the meadow, and I turned a cartwheel, just for the freedom of summer. Luke somersaulted.

I turned to tell him to catch up, when a strange sign sticking out of the shop front lawn caught my eye. Something about the sign didn't seem right. Sometimes Mom tacked up a notice outside the shop saying SPECIAL: HAM AND CHEESE, $4.99 or EXTRAORDINARY PIES INSIDE. But this sign didn't say anything like that. In fact, it didn't seem like something Mom would put out.

"What's 'Take Back Vermont' mean?" Luke asked, standing next to me.

"I don't know," I said. Right away I knew it wasn't right; it wasn't something Mom or Eva had posted.

"We should ask MJ if she wants it there."

I shivered. Someone had been sneaking around early, hammering the sign outside our shop.

We were still standing there when Eva pulled out of the driveway. She tooted her horn, and Mom came out to wave. But then suddenly Eva was out of the car, running, and Mom ran, too. They were running toward the sign. Eva got to it first, and in one angry motion, she pulled out the stake and ripped the sign in half. She looked around wildly, but Mom grabbed her and pulled her close. I turned away.

"Let's go," I said to Luke.

chapter two

THE FOREST WAS cool, and Luke and I moved silently. After the meadow, the needles underfoot felt good, although it took a certain talent to walk barefoot in the brush. We stepped over broken branches, avoiding pine cones and brambles.

Good thing my feet knew what to do, because my head was full of stormy thoughts. Eva was embarrassing me again. It was just a sign, wasn't it? The way she looked — red and irrational — was just like that day at the softball game. Except then everybody had been watching. And everybody had heard Eva yell at Lauren's mother. And Tina — my best friend — had stood next to Lauren, staring at me.

I breathed in the smell of cedar and forced my thoughts back to berries. I concentrated on the small flowers around me, spotting not blueberry but blackberry blooms that would ripen in a month. Bleeding hearts and fiddle-head ferns pushed up around the rotting logs and moss-covered rocks.

"Come on," Luke said. "This is a really cool place."

The main trail was wide and clear behind the old camp, but as we climbed higher, the trail dwindled. New shoots sprouted where no one had stepped in a long time. Wherever the sun pierced through, a tangle of birch seedlings, briars, and cornflowers reached for the light. Blueberries needed sun, too; the rocky soil was a good sign.

"This way," Luke said, and pushed aside a low branch.

It was a faded trail — perhaps just a fox path — but you could see it if you knew what to look for: snapped branches, scuffed-aside leaves, bent seedlings.

The trail curved along the cliff's edge. We were maybe twenty or thirty feet above the lake, and I was careful where I put my feet.

Luke stopped and waved his hands like a magician. "Ta-da!"

All around us were low bushes with tiny leaves and light green fruit. I studied them for any hint of blue.

"Not yet," I said. "But soon." Holding on to a branch, I smiled into the sun. My toes warmed on the rocky cliff's edge.

"That's not all, though," Luke said. He stripped off his shirt and walked to the edge.

I took a small step closer. It was easily thirty feet down. My hands got damp just thinking about how high up we were. A pine leaned over, its roots like octopus tentacles clinging to the dirt. I looked again—I didn't want Luke to think I was a wimp. Six feet below was a worn-down ledge, like a diving platform. And beyond that, a narrow, jagged way to climb back up from the water.

"I checked it out from the boat," Luke said. "The water is forty feet deep, and there are no rocks."

"You going to jump?"

"Yeah," he said. "You, too."

"I don't know about that." Jumping off the low rocks around Luke's island was one thing, but this was different. The water would hurt, like hitting pavement.

"Come on," Luke said. He started down to the ledge. "Sometimes you just have to go for it."

As Luke reached the jumping spot, the sound of voices broke beyond the trees. Sam Costa, Tina's older brother, and a couple of his friends came down the trail, yelling and shoving each other. I backed away from the edge.

"Hey, look who's here," said Sam. "Luke and June."

"Where's Tina?" I asked.

"Home watching Tim and the farm stand," he said, kicking off his sneakers. "Aren't you kids too little to go cliff jumping?"

"No way," Luke said. I didn't say anything.

"Go on, then," Sam said. "Jump!"

Luke looked back up at me and grinned. He would have jumped anyway, but now he would go down in style.

Luke gave a war whoop and jumped, waving his arms and legs. The boys hollered, too. I watched Luke's splash, holding my breath. Then he surfaced, shook hair out of his eyes, and yelled, "Awesome!"

Sam climbed down to the ledge for his turn and waited for Luke to climb back up. I leaned back against a tree. Why did these guys have to come along? If Tina had come too, she would have known how to handle her brother's teasing. Except maybe I couldn't count on her to stand up for me anymore. I scratched a mosquito bite on my leg.

Luke pulled himself up to the top. "Don't you want to try it?" He shook his wet hair.

"Not this time." I moved farther back.

"Aw, come on," Sam said. "You chicken?"

"I just don't feel like it."

"What a lezzie," one of the other boys said.

I stiffened.

"That would be her moms," snorted Sam.

Their loud laughter landed like a punch. *I only have one mom,* I wanted to say.

"Hey, knock it off," Luke said.

"Don't worry, man," Sam said. "We're going to take back Vermont."

Take back Vermont? I was shaking and red-faced. What did it mean?

"Better think again." Luke snapped up his shirt.

"Vermont doesn't belong to anyone!" I stepped toward Sam, as close to the cliff's edge as I dared.

He didn't flinch. "No freaks allowed."

"Let's go," Luke said. He grabbed my clenched fist and held on.

With my arm stretched like a lifeline to his, we moved fast, shoving branches, crashing over logs. I was glad for the dark woods. Sweat ran down my face, and I wished I had jumped, jumped into the cool lake, away from Sam.

It was like the end of sixth grade again and the softball game that had turned me into an outcast. Lauren had called someone "gay," and Mom told her not to use that word, and Lauren's mother said, *"Don't tell my child what to do,"* and then Eva yelled, *"We won't keep quiet about homophobia"* and Lauren's mother yelled, *"Stay out of our lives, stay out of our bedroom!"* And then Eva just had to say, *"As if what happens in our bedroom affects yours"* — and I wanted to die.

That was when a line had been drawn. You were either for gay people or against them. Mom and Eva and I had looked like the players nobody wanted on their team. Lauren and Tina were on the popular side, that's for sure. I remembered, too, that Mom and Eva had been stunned by the silence. Nobody said anything, not even Tina's mother. I had thought she was Mom's friend — they were always talking about teachers, going together to PTA meetings. It didn't make sense.

Everything had been easier before Eva moved in. When Mom needed a break, it was Joe who came over and played Chutes and Ladders with me, and Monopoly, too. Sometimes he'd bring over sheets of butcher-block paper and we'd draw. I'd add eyes to his interlocking swirls and lines. And then he'd give them funny names like Impatience and Confused, and make up stories about our drawings. I was usually asleep by the time Mom got home; it never mattered who she was with. But then Luke's mom had moved out, and Joe was around less. And then Mom met Eva.

I dropped Luke's hand to slap mosquitoes away. What did "Take Back Vermont" mean? Someone had been angry enough to plant a sign in front of our shop. Luke didn't think that way, though. I suddenly missed his hand in mine.

Luke fell in step next to me. "Don't let those guys bug you. That's just talk."

I pictured Lauren's mother's angry face. "What about the sign?"

"Maybe it means the Abenaki are going to take Vermont back from us white men."

I looked at him strangely.

"Or"—he slapped a branch away—"Vermont's got to go back to the days of no electricity and wood-burning stoves."

I started to catch on. "No, it means let's take Vermont back to when everybody had to grow their own food and shovel snow by hand."

"Let's go back to the days of outhouses!" shouted Luke. "A ban on indoor plumbing!"

I laughed. "That's it! That's what they want! No more toilets and hot tubs!"

"We'll have to wash in the lake," he said. "Race you!"

We broke into a run across the meadow.

Blue lights flashing outside the marina stopped us.

"What happened?" Luke asked.

A cop was talking to Mom and Eva. Joe was there, too, looking sleepy. Mom must have motored over and woken him up.

"Oh, June, there you are," Mom said, and pulled me in for a hug.

"You were worried?" Luke and I always went wherever we wanted. "You said come back at lunch."

"I did, I did." But Mom didn't let go.

"What's going on?" Luke asked.

"Thank you for your time." Eva was shaking the police officer's hand.

"We'll keep an eye on things," he said.

Joe patted Luke on the back. "You go home and let

these gals talk things over. I'll watch the shop for a bit," he said to Mom and Eva. "Remember, I'm just a boat ride away."

It was strange enough that Eva hadn't gone to work — we'd been gone an hour at least. Even now she didn't seem to be in any hurry. Why hadn't she gone? Why didn't she just leave Mom and me alone, instead of causing a scene? I turned back and watched Luke row out to their island. Suddenly, I wished I had stayed on the stool in the marina shop, just selling sandwiches and pie.

chapter three

"WHERE WERE YOU?" Eva demanded once we got inside.

I turned to Mom. "Who's asking?"

"We worry, that's all." Mom dropped her arm from around Eva. "You didn't see anybody, anything strange?"

"We were up by the old camp," I said. I kept quiet about the cliff jumping.

Like a sixth sense, Mom seemed to know. "You're a long way up from the lake on that trail," she said. "Be careful you don't slip."

"June is not the problem," Eva said. She rubbed her hands. "Last spring, and now this —"

"We're OK," Mom said, catching Eva's hands. "No one's hurt, and that's all that matters."

"This time," Eva said.

"Why were the police here?" I asked.

Mom let go of Eva and dragged a flat of berries onto the table. "Here, let's cut up these strawberries." She handed me a knife and began hulling and slicing them. I stood there for a moment, knife in hand, and watched them. No one was going to answer my question.

Eva unfolded the newspaper. "There's another head-line, MJ."

Mom nodded. "Things may get worse before they get better."

"If they get better," Eva said.

I didn't sit down. "What's going to get worse?"

Eva folded the newspaper again and put it in the basket on the table. "A lot of people are angry since the law allowing same-gender couples to hold civil ceremonies went into effect in July."

I stabbed my knife into a strawberry. "I didn't think you cared what other people thought."

"June." Mom motioned for me to sit. "Chop."

I sat down and began thwacking the blade on the cutting board.

Eva smoothed her hair behind her ears. "Some people are trying to elect new senators and even a governor who would repeal the law."

"They want to erase the law, in a sense," Mom explained.

"Let them," I said. The law made people angry. I had

seen it twice—once at the softball game, and now with Sam.

"You don't mean that," Mom said, and Eva chimed in, "It's important to us."

To you, I thought, but didn't say it out loud. I sliced another strawberry. "What does 'Take Back Vermont' mean?"

"I was hoping you hadn't seen that sign," Mom said.

"I'm not a baby."

Mom set down her knife. "Some people think Vermont will be taken over by gay people if this law remains. They want Vermont to be just for Vermonters, not outsiders."

"We *are* Vermonters," I said.

"That's the point," Eva said.

"Did you call the police?" I asked Mom.

"We had to report the sign."

"That's not all." Eva paced by the window. "We found a note on the car about how lesbians shouldn't be allowed to raise children."

"Eva!" Mom said. She gave my hand a squeeze. "That's why I was afraid for you. But don't worry about it, June."

I held on. "You're my mom." She'd given birth to me. No one could change that. But I knew who the problem was. It didn't surprise me that Eva was looking out the window.

I sliced a large strawberry fast. When it was just Mom

and me, I used to pretend I had a dad who was a salesman, always away. Later, I understood that Mom went out on dates with special friends, and sometimes I met them. But no one lasted. Not until Eva. I threw the strawberry pieces into the bowl. The dad story ended the day Eva moved in. It had been one month, and nothing seemed better.

Mom took my hand and held it tight. "I always told you that I chose you — that I wanted to raise a child even though I wasn't going to marry a man."

I nodded. It was a familiar story.

"And now I've chosen Eva, too," she said softly.

"You told me."

"We've chosen each other," Eva said, moving next to Mom, their smiles matching.

"What about me?" I stood up.

"We're a family now." Mom pulled me close. "Honey, we weren't going to tell you until later, but we've talked about it. We'd like to have a civil union ceremony."

"The new law protects us," Eva said, "and especially you."

I pulled back, not listening. "You want to get married?"

That meant Eva was going to be with us always. Tidying up around the kitchen, talking endlessly about politics, nosing into my life. Would there be a picture in the newspaper? I imagined Lauren snickering in the hall at school, *I saw your moms' wedding announcement, con-*

gratulations. And who did they think would come besides Luke's dad? Nobody wanted to see two women kissing — not even their friends. Kissing — anyone — was something I couldn't think about right now.

"We can talk about the wedding later," Eva said. "What's more important is your safety." Her pager buzzed. "I've got to go. You two be careful, OK?"

"We're just making pies," I said. "Like we always do."

Mom and I kept hulling and slicing strawberries, our knives thudding together.

"No worries, OK?" Mom said, adjusting her glasses on her nose. "We asked Joe if he had heard or seen anything last night, but he hadn't. Someone is trying to scare us, but we think it was some kids who didn't know what they were doing was illegal."

No worries, right. It was an old game of ours, but there was plenty to worry about. The thought of the note and sign as a prank didn't make me feel better. It could have been Sam. He knew exactly what this was about. But he wouldn't go to the trouble — he had been planning to go cliff jumping, right? Yet imagining a grownup sneaking around was even worse.

My head ached, and Mom's silence seeped into me so I couldn't speak. When the bell dinged down at the marina shop, I jumped up to take Joe's place.

"Hey, June, maybe you can try a little harder to be friendly to Eva," Mom added. I rolled my eyes.

I WAS EDGY all afternoon, suspicious of everyone who came into the store. Was there a way to tell if someone hated gay people or not? The way they held their change or chose apple pie instead of raspberry-strawberry? A man from the New York side of the lake bought some gas. Three French Canadians sailed down from Montreal and wanted picnic supplies. They bought two wrapped cookies.

Slowly, after selling marine maps, oil, full pies and slices, I stopped worrying. Most people just saw a kid working the cash register. They didn't know about Mom and Eva. But I couldn't get the picture of their wedding out of my head. If Mom and Eva had a civil union ceremony, then everybody would know.

Mom finally relieved me in the shop, and I jumped into the lake. I swam hard, washing away all the anxiety of the day, only coming up for air every four strokes. Dusk is the best time on the lake—when the calm often returns and the water turns inky black. The sun was casting its last light on Luke's island and the Green Mountains beyond. I floated on my back, thinking of my small self in this giant lake, all one hundred and ten miles of it. It was holding me, gently, like a hug from a friend.

I didn't notice Luke until his rowboat was almost on top of me.

"Watch where you're going," he said. "I almost ran over you!"

"Watch yourself." I rocked his boat.

"Hey!" he shouted, and pretended to fall in. We splashed each other and dove for rocks, letting his boat drift in the shallow water.

"This one's perfect for skipping." Luke flicked the flat stone hard. We watched it skim three, four, five times.

"Watch this."

"Not bad," he said as it bounced three times.

For a while we were silent, scooping up rocks and skipping them.

"I heard Mrs. Costa's entering her pies, too," he said.

"At the fair?" I thought of her professional farm stand pies—she won a ribbon every year. "But I'll be in the kids' section, anyway. We won't be competing."

"Her pies are pretty good," Luke said.

"Not as good as mine!" An idea crept into my mind. To win the kids' division, I'd have to be as good as Mrs. Costa. Their farm produced the best strawberries, and Mrs. Costa probably used homemade butter in the crust, churned from cow's milk.

"Maybe we should go visit Tina," Luke said as if reading my mind. "Do some sampling of her mom's pies— compare notes."

"I don't know," I said. "Tina and I aren't really friends right now."

He skipped another rock. "You don't think Sam had anything to do with the sign, do you?"

I shook my head. Even though I'd wondered, too, it was hard to imagine.

"C'mon—I'll flash my green light tomorrow when I'm ready to go," he said, climbing back into his boat. Then he paused. "I'll look for your red light if there's trouble, OK?"

"Pie trouble, you mean?"

He grinned. "I'll row right over."

"Thanks." I watched his oars turn as he rowed home. Neither of us had ordinary families—how many kids live without a car or phone on an island?—but mine took the prize. I turned from the lake and walked up to the house. Through the kitchen window, I could see Mom and Eva preparing dinner together. Mom was smiling while Eva talked. I closed my eyes and wished it were just the two of us again. Then I could pretend my parents were divorced and that my dad was on the road, selling stuff, and everyone would leave us alone.

chapter four

THE NEXT MORNING, the lake was frenzied, all chop-
py and wavy. I rested my head on my hands and watched
the water crash against the shore, battering it. Just like the
angry words crashing around in my head.

Downstairs, I could hear Eva talking about the wedding, about whether black-eyed Susans would be better
than Queen Anne's lace on every table. Mom was too
busy; I could tell. She was saying *uh huh* to everything as
if she cared.

I flicked on my weather radio to drown out Eva's voice.
"Today, northwest wind five to ten knots, waves around
one foot," the announcer said in his gravelly voice. "The
Lake Champlain lake level at the King Street ferry dock is
ninety-six point six feet. The water temperature is sixty-
seven degrees. Chance of afternoon showers."

It was comforting to hear the weatherman say what I

could see—clouds low, waves crashing. Maybe it was a good day to make plans for the Champlain Valley Fair pie competition. I let my mind fill with memories of pies —ones I'd made and those I'd had from Mrs. Costa's farm stand. I examined my fingertips, still faintly red from hulling strawberries the day before. Maybe I'd make strawberry-rhubarb tonight. Maybe Luke was right—I could get some ideas from Mrs. Costa.

I turned away from the water and stared at the ceiling. No way did I want to go visit Tina, not even for pie re-search. Even with Luke with me, I didn't want to run into her brother.

The only person I wanted to see was Luke. I looked out the window, but his signal was yellow. I got up and clambered down out of the loft.

"Good morning, June," Mom said from the breakfast table. Eva was filling her travel mug with coffee. "Luke dropped by to say he and his father were heading into Burlington all day."

So much for doing something with my one friend. I popped a slice of bread in the toaster.

"Shelly called," Mom said.

"Mrs. Costa?"

"Yes, Mrs. Costa." Mom looked at me. "She said she needs some sixteen-plait running rigging. I told her you could bike some over today."

"Won't that be too heavy?" Eva asked. "I could drive."

Mom and I exchanged a look. "It's just rope," she explained.

I took a bite of toast. I didn't want to go without Luke. "Don't you need me at the marina?"

"I need you to run this errand to the Costas." Mom put her arm around my shoulders. "I hope you're not hiding from your friend, just because grownups disagree sometimes."

I didn't say anything, flushing at the memory of Tina's silence after Eva's outburst. Obviously, Mom and Mrs. Costa were talking again, although I couldn't see how. Mom and Eva had been really mad at her after the softball game. Tina and I hadn't talked at all.

Mom handed me my backpack. "Shelly said Tina is going to enter Moonbeam in the fair this year."

Last year it was Sam who had entered a calf, his father patting him on the back, guiding him. Tina and I had just hung around, too young to participate. It was our turn now. She would be in the dairy animals category and I would be in the culinary arts. Maybe it would be OK. Maybe we could talk about the fair and not about families.

I put on the backpack. "Did you pick up the entry form for the competition?"

"Not yet," Mom said.

"I'm going to make the best pie ever," I said as I banged out the door on the way to the marina to get the rigging.

● ● ●

IT WAS A short bike ride to the Costa Farm, along the shore, past the town, and then north. Once I left the lake, the day was muggy and hot, and my pedaling slowed. I wasn't in a hurry to get there, which gave me plenty of time to think. I hadn't talked to Tina since the game. I missed talking to her. She was probably busy around the farm, though, taking care of Moonbeam. I had been busy, too, so maybe that was why we hadn't called each other.

By the time I reached the farm, I was dying for a drink, and I had convinced myself that if Mom and Mrs. Costa were talking, then everything would be fine between Tina and me.

"Good to see you, June," Mrs. Costa said from behind the farm stand counter. She sounded as if she meant it. "Do you have the rigging?"

I took it out of my backpack. "Mom said we'll put it on your tab."

"Are you sure?"

I nodded.

"You tell her that's very kind," Mrs. Costa said. "Tina, take a break and give June some lemonade in the kitchen."

Tina was weighing a bag of potatoes for a customer. Our summer differences were already showing. I was lake-wet almost all the time, and Tina was dusty-freckled, although her pink nail polish sparkled as her fingers punched the register keys.

"That's three ninety-five, please." Tina hefted the bag over the counter. She was a wiz on the cash register, just like me. When we were in second grade, our teacher had been amazed with our speedy adding and subtracting.

"I want to check on Moonbeam first," Tina said. "C'mon." She disappeared out the back door of the stand.

The barn was dark, cool, and quiet. Moonbeam's hide shone like a light in the corner of his stall. He was chewing quietly.

"Isn't he beautiful?" Tina said. "I weighed him this morning and he's thirteen hundred and sixty-two pounds. That's champion-size." She entered the stall with a brush in hand. Moonbeam turned around to nuzzle her. I climbed up on the rail — no need to get too close to something thirteen times heavier than me.

I was quiet as Tina worked on Moonbeam, grateful that she hadn't mentioned Eva's craziness. It felt like old times.

"I hope you win," I said. "Did you hear I'm entering the pie competition?"

"Maybe we'll both get blue ribbons," she said. "What are you going to make?"

"I can't decide. What's your mom making?"

"Strawberry, probably." Tina brushed Moonbeam's

flank. "Whatever you do, I know it will be the best. My mom said the other day you make good pies."

"She did?" Liking my pies was the same as liking me and my family, wasn't it? "I think hers are good, too."

"All Moonbeam needs is water. Then let's go to the kitchen and see what's left."

Tina handed me the hose and turned the water on. I filled up Moonbeam's water trough and cooled myself down with a quick splash on my head. I shook my hair out like a wet dog as we walked up to the main house.

The kitchen was full of brothers—Tim eating a slice of pie and Sam pouring milk.

"Look who walked in—did you fall in the lake?" Sam asked. "Or jump? Oh wait, you're too chicken."

I flushed and started to snap back, but Tina spoke first.

"What are you talking about? June lives in the lake." Tina took down two glasses and poured us both some lemonade. "I've never been over to her house when we didn't end up in the water."

"Anyway, I'll jump someday." I shot Tina a grateful glance.

"I'm going out to help Dad." Sam bonked Tina on the head. "Tag, you're it, for Tim duty."

Tina sliced up two pieces of strawberry pie, then washed Tim's hands and face. "You go and play," she said to him. "I'll find you in a minute."

We took a long swig of lemonade and came up for air at the same time, which made us giggle.

"You're lucky you don't have brothers," she said. "Summer is more work than school."

"I made six dozen cookies last week." I wanted to make peace. "But it sure beats listening to grownups lose it."

"Yeah, my parents have been acting a little weird lately, too."

Truce, maybe.

Tina balanced a bite on her fork. "Where did you see Sam?"

"Promise not to tell?"

She nodded.

"Luke and I found a great new spot with wild blueberries. They're not ripe yet, but I'm going back in a week," I said. "The berries are right on the edge of a cliff, along the trail up from the old camp. It's a cliff-jumping spot. When we were there, Sam and some other guys came."

"Did they all jump?"

I nodded.

"I'd never do that—I'm too afraid of heights," she said.

"Me, too." But remembering the cliff's edge didn't make me stiffen as much as remembering the hateful words her brother had said. I couldn't tell Tina, not now that everything seemed regular between us again. I ate another mouthful.

"What do you think?" Tina asked, her lips red with berry juice.

"It's great, as usual," I said. The crust was the best — flaky and rich, and it held together nicely because of their homemade butter. "I may have to ask for some of your butter."

"I was talking about my lips!" she said, making a kissing face.

I grinned and smeared some strawberry filling on mine.

"Beautiful, dahling," she said.

When it was time to go, I waved to Tina, feeling lighter than I had in a long time. I pushed my kickstand up and strapped on my helmet. A light rain had started. Just as I turned the farm stand corner, I heard Mr. Costa say, "Yeah, we're going to take it back."

I couldn't see who he was talking to, and I didn't turn around. My insides just congealed a little, like a pie left out overnight.

chapter five

WHEN EVERYTHING GETS muddled up inside my head, there's nothing better than making pies. Mom came back from her evening sail and set me up with flour, butter, and the big bowls. The strawberries were sliced and ready to go. Rhubarb stalks were washed and stacked next to a bowl of peaches.

"What's it going to be, pie maker?" Eva said, putting away the last dinner plate.

I washed my hands, my back to her. "Maybe strawberry-peach or peach-rhubarb."

"Whatever kind you make will be perfect," Eva said.

I turned to Mom, annoyed. "How many should I make?" I dipped my hands in the flour.

Eva went into the office, and Mom looked uncomfortable. "As many as you feel like," she said. "I'll do more later. We'll be doing the accounting, OK?"

I began to fill the measuring cup, but Mom lingered, watching me. I was sorry she wouldn't be helping. I had made my first pie when I was six with leftover dough scraps she had given me. I used to pat the dough down, sprinkle it with cinnamon sugar, and Mom baked it for a snack. But that time, I had shaped the dough into a cup like a tart and begged for a few apples for filling.

"No worries, right, June bug?" Mom asked.

I smiled. She hadn't called me June bug in a long time.

"I know things are hard right now," she said. "Everything OK with Tina?"

I nodded. I didn't say anything about Mr. Costa.

"Change is hard sometimes, but good, too," she added. "Eva's just excited, hoping the rest of the world under-stands us."

"What if Vermont is not ready?" I asked. *Or me,* I thought. But I felt a little bad for ignoring Eva again.

"Don't worry about it. You just do what you do best." She ruffled my hair. "Making pies."

I dumped in eight cups of flour to start a quadruple recipe of pie crust: two cups flour, thirteen tablespoons of butter, a teaspoon salt, and a quarter cup water times four. Once I had guessed the measurements, but I had learned to do it precisely to avoid sticky or dry crust.

I clicked the knives against each other, cutting the but-ter into the flour. Pie making can be good thinking time.

Right now I didn't know what to think except that I wasn't interested in change, not the Eva kind.

I worked the dough with my hands, stealing a smidge of salty, flour-coated butter. Finally the dough held together, and I formed four balls.

"Knock, knock," Luke said through the screen.

"Want to make pies?" I waved my floured hands.

"Why not? My dad's not needing me."

I handed Luke a rolling pin and we began rolling dough under wax paper.

"I went to the Costas' today," I said.

"And . . ."

"Well, Mrs. Costa's real butter makes a difference in her crust."

"Not surprising," he said. "What else?"

"Moonbeam practically glows, Tina keeps him so clean," I said. "She's entering him in the fair."

"Any trouble?" Luke swung the rolling pin like a bat.

I pretended he was scaring me. "No."

Then I was quiet for a minute and told him what I had heard Mr. Costa say. "They seemed friendly like always," I said. "I just can't see them being nice and then hating Mom and Eva inside."

Luke began working on the next ball of dough. "We saw a lot of those 'Take Back Vermont' signs in Burlington. It could have been anyone."

"A lot?"

"We also saw some 'Keep It Civil' signs."

"I just want the whole thing to disappear." I pressed the crusts into the pie plates and began measuring the sugar and the flour for the fruit. This is the part that takes talent. I tasted the strawberries. They were sweet but a little tart. The rhubarb is always sour, so I added a little more sugar. Lemon never hurts either.

As soon as the sugar and flour were mixed in, the juices started flowing. I scooped the fruit into the shells and licked my fingers.

Luke smeared his whole palm in the bowl and began licking his hand. "Got anything else to eat around here?"

"Is that you, Luke?" Mom called from the office. "Did your dad forget about dinner again? I was thinking you guys might like the leftover sandwiches from the shop. We didn't sell too many today."

"We'd love 'em," he said.

"I'm almost done." I sealed one of the pies with my two fingers and thumb. I fluted the edges of the last ones and placed them in the oven.

Outside, the evening was warm. A breeze kept most of the mosquitoes away.

"Race you to the shop," I said. Luke took off and passed me in a second. It felt good, flying through the darkness toward the shop's light.

Inside, we found five sandwiches. "That means Mom sold only about ten sandwiches today," I said, surprised. There were even cookies left over, so I grabbed one.

"More for me!" He scooped the sandwiches into his arms.

We sat on the dock, looking out at the lake. The sky was turning pink and purple as the sun set. It gave the trees a warm hue, setting Luke's island aglow. Luke unwrapped a ham and cheese, and I thought about him not eating dinner with Joe. I guess if a sculpture idea grabs you, you don't remember dinner. If I had a dad, I'd make him come and eat with me.

"Sometimes," I said, taking a bite of a cookie, "I wonder if I eat like my father."

Luke looked at me chewing. "You mean like a pig?"

I punched Luke in the leg. "No, like if he chews fast or takes a drink between every bite, that kind of thing."

"You're crazy."

I looked at him. Luke's mother probably ate French cuisine every night at the Quebec hotel she managed. "Do you think my father likes pie?" I persisted.

"Everybody likes pie," he said. "Especially yours."

"Yeah, well, I wouldn't know if he's ever eaten one," I said, feeling sorry for myself. All I knew—all Mom knew—was my father was a New Yorker and a sperm donor. I kicked the water.

Luke's hand covered mine then, on the dock. I felt a flush of heat, like last time by the cliff. *I'm on your side,* his hand told me.

Maybe I was imagining things. Next thing I knew, he was pulling me into the lake.

"Hey!" I said, whipping my wet hair out of my eyes. I splashed him, and he splashed back until we both had to duck under.

The lake was black, like a cool coat around me. I wasn't afraid of the dark bottom, and I relaxed in the water's quiet embrace.

When I came up for air, Luke was by the dock. A low gong had sounded across the lake. Joe must have finished for the night.

"Gotta go." Luke put the rest of the sandwiches in the dinghy, and I untied the boat for him.

I watched him row. Luke and I, we were in the same boat with these missing parents. I headed back up to the house.

"I just don't think getting married right after the law passes is such a good idea." Mom's voice pierced the night. Instantly, I sank below the open kitchen window, against the side of the house.

"Why not? We should celebrate our relationship." Eva's voice rose. "It's the right thing to do. And there's June to consider."

"That's who I'm thinking of," Mom said. "Someone has already threatened to take her away."

My breathing sharpened. Every muscle stilled.

"You're exaggerating." Eva sounded exasperated. "The note said 'shouldn't have children,' not——"

"That's where it starts . . ."

"All the more reason to make it legal, then, to make her *our* child," Eva said.

"June does not need us to draw attention to our relationship right now," Mom said.

"You sound ashamed of us——"

"Ashamed!?" Mom's voice was tight with anger. "Eva, I'm being practical, realistic! By getting married in a civil ceremony, June could be teased or worse by her classmates. Just like last spring at the game."

"She went to Tina's today. They'll be friends again in no time."

"That's just one friend," Mom said. "And what about the business? We've already lost customers. Let's let this blow over."

"Why? Getting married now won't change anything —it'll still be a 'lesbian shop.'"

"Maybe it's OK in your Burlington job, but not here!" Every word Mom spoke came out hard. "These are my neighbors. I will not hide, but I don't need to parade my politics in front of them."

It was silent then in the kitchen, and I pressed my eyes closed. Could someone really take me away from my mom? Could it be true that not as many people wanted our sandwiches and cookies and pies because Eva had moved in? And as much as that scared me, the silence in the kitchen scared me more. I'd never heard Mom and Eva fight before. I began shivering.

And then an unmistakable smell filled my nostrils.

"The pies are burning!" Mom shouted. *"June!"*

I rushed in the kitchen, but it was too late.

"How could you forget them?" Mom pulled the four scorched pies from the oven. The fire alarm screamed, and Eva reached up to take the battery out.

"You even forgot to cover the edges. These are useless."

"I'm sorry," I whispered. I couldn't remember the last time I had made a mistake.

"June, I don't want you to enter the fair," Mom said decisively.

I stared at her. "I won't burn them again, I promise."

"It's just not a good time, June, for you to be —"

"You said I was ready." I looked at Mom in disbelief.

"Let's talk about it another day," Eva said, resting her hands on Mom's shoulders. "Let's go to bed."

Mom shrugged Eva's hands away. "Not me — I've got a lot of work to do if we're going to have any sweets to sell in the shop tomorrow."

"Can I help?" I asked.

"Not tonight, honey."

Up in my loft, I pulled the covers over my head. And even though the kitchen was not far, it felt like the space between us had expanded. Mom wanted to be alone, and that scared me.

chapter six

THE SMELL OF burned pie seemed to linger for days. No breeze kicked off from the lake to blow things over, and the water lay as flat as I felt. I mean, who cared if I wasn't registered for the fair; maybe I wasn't the best pie maker. I was absolutely becalmed, and no one seemed to notice.

Everything was fine before Eva. I pulled my blanket tight around me and stared out at the water. How could she accuse Mom of being ashamed? No one would take me away from here, away from Mom. We were Vermonters, not Eva. She was barging into our lives, pushing her politics. If only she hadn't said anything at that softball game, then Lauren's mom wouldn't have yelled, *"Don't talk to my kid — stay out of our lives, stay out of our bedroom!"* I squeezed my eyes shut, forcing the angry words out of my mind. I didn't like hearing the argument last night, either. A tiny hope flourished that maybe Eva would leave, but I immediately felt guilty for wishing it.

When I opened my eyes again, it had started to rain. I watched the widening circles each raindrop made on the lake, overlapping and dimpling the surface. Everything was gray but also refreshed. Maybe the rain would wash away the smell of burned pies.

But it wouldn't change one thing. I stood on my chair and pulled down a cardboard box from the top of my closet. Its edges were worn and the flaps were permanently creased. It was easy to open. I did it gently, as I had many many times. I picked up the card first, with pink and purple balloons and the words *Happy Birthday* in block, little-kid letters.

Dear June, welcome, my daughter. I am writing this on your Birth Day to tell you that I wanted you — I chose to have you on my own because I have so much love to give you. I love you, your mother.

I fingered the hospital bracelet, the tiny footprint on the paper with the pink bow. She told me that she wrote the card right after I had my first feeding. When I was little, I asked Mom to go over everything in the box, every night.

I pulled out *It's so Amazing!* and flipped through the pages of cartoons describing eggs and sperms. I used to look at it alone, reviewing the ways families are made. It was the only book that talked about the way I was born. The other book in the box was *Heather Has Two Mommies*. I used to ask Mom to read it over and over. She had been trying to explain that she wanted one of the "special friends" she went out with to have a more permanent part in her life. Now it meant only one thing: I would never have a father.

I opened the brown envelope. *Margaret Jane Farrell* was written at the top of a faded copy of a long form. Age: *39*. Reason for admittance: *donor insemination*. And then, the information about the sperm donor Number 58362. Birthplace: *New York, New York*. Education: *Columbia University*. Age: *26*. *No known diseases*.

I looked out the window as the rain gathered on the glass. Somewhere, a man was taking subways in New York, going to work. I imagined him wearing glasses, his dark head bent over newspapers. His ears must be small like mine, because Mom's were different. Maybe he was married. Maybe I had brothers or sisters out there.

Mom had wanted a family. And so my mother had chosen him, and me. And now she had chosen Eva. Or had she changed her mind?

I turned on my flashlight, placing a green lens over it. I looked through the binoculars to Luke's house. No light yet. I shifted my view to the marina shop. Mom was already there. Downstairs, I heard shuffling and clinking cups. I waited until a door opened and closed. A car started up. Eva was going to work.

I sighed. I probably needed to help Mom at the shop today. But maybe Luke was around. I put on my bathing suit, grabbed a banana, and headed down to the lake.

● ● ●

PADDLING IN THE rain is different. I checked the sky: light gray, soft rain. Good, that meant lightning was unlikely. I lifted my face and let the rain mat my hair to my forehead. Bathing suits are perfect for rainy days. My paddle sliced the water, swirling eddies behind the canoe. The rhythm of each stroke was a familiar song.

I tied up my boat to Luke's dock and walked toward the sculpture on shore. Until you got used to it, the large eye tangled in wavy metal rods was unnerving. But I liked Joe's art. It looked like the eye of the sun watching the horizon line, peeking through skinny trees.

"Hello!" I called.

"Over here!"

The studio, of course. Joe was standing in the open door of the garage he had built on the island. It was funny to see a garage on an island with no cars or roads, but of course the inside was not for a car: it was full of large and small bits of metal and machinery. When Joe was in the middle of something, sparks would be flying and you had to stand back. But sometimes you'd find him at the butcher-block kitchen counter, drawing sketches of what he was imagining next. Those moments were the ones I liked, when Luke and I would sit around, listening to him philosophize.

Today he was leaning an eight-foot sculpture toward him while Luke walked around it with bubble wrap.

"Sold something?"

"Just taking a few pieces to the gallery." Joe pointed to the base of the sculpture. "Luke, make sure you get some around the feet."

The metal spikes ended in waves and right angles at the top. It looked like lake weed that had been run over by a motorboat. "What's this one called?"

"Pathfinder."

Luke grinned. "I wanted to name it *Twisted Sister.*"

"That makes you Crazy Brother." I dodged Luke's poke. "Can you swim today?"

"Luke has to help unload in Burlington." Joe turned to me. "Do you want to come?"

"I'm going to help Mom during lunch." I didn't say it with much enthusiasm.

Joe studied my face and then the rain-splattered lake. "Well, if you two want to do a little swimming before we go, there's time."

Luke was off. "I'll get my suit on!"

Joe threw a tarp over the wrapped sculpture. "Can you carry this with me down to the motorboat?"

"Sure." It was heavy, but I could do it. Joe walked carefully backwards, holding the base while I carried the top. His eyes took in the worry lines around my eyes.

"What's up, June?"

I shrugged.

"It's hard when someone new moves in," he observed. "I remember when Camille first lived out here, we had to learn a whole new way of being together."

"But she left," I blurted out.

Joe walked out on the dock, slowly lowering his end into the boat. He gestured to me to set my end down in the bow. His eye traveled across the bay to the marina shop. "I don't think Eva's leaving, if you're worried. Or hoping." He grinned. "She and MJ are a good pair. Maybe it's hard to see."

"They're different." I tucked the tarp down around the metal piece to keep the rain off.

"True," he said. "Eva's not much of a sailor."

"That's not what I meant." I scowled. "She's not much of a dad, either."

"Trying to be a father would put extra pressure on a gal, that's for sure." He tried to joke, but I didn't smile. "If you're looking for guy talk, you can always chat with me."

I nodded. Once I had hoped Mom and Joe would marry. It seemed silly now.

Luke came running down to the dock and right off the edge, into the water. Joe and I both laughed.

"Go swim," Joe said. "Everything will be OK."

Luke climbed up the path to the granite rock at the tip of the island. "Come on, June! Practice jumping off these rocks."

"Piece of cake." I clambered up next to him. These rocks were only five or six feet above the water. It was easy; I had leapt before.

"Piece of pie, you mean!" Luke cannonballed.

"Cowabunga!" I hollered, and followed him in. My heart fluttered only for a moment before I landed. The lake was warm compared to the rainy air, and I sprang back to the surface.

We jumped about ten more times. And it was true — each jump was easier. All the while, Joe was watching us. *That's what dads do,* I thought. And it was nice to think of him as a pretend father, but it wasn't quite the same as the real thing.

chapter seven

BY THE TIME I finished the lunch shift at Stillwater Marina, the rain had stopped. Mom and I had worked in companionable silence, but I could tell we were walking around the big things worrying us. I kept thinking about the Costas, and about the "Take Back Vermont" sign. And I wondered if the wedding was still on.

Mom closed the cover on another paperback and set her glasses high on her nose. Plenty of time to read; it was slow for lunchtime. I counted the sandwiches again: fifteen to start, and there were still ten left.

It was probably the smell of burned pies keeping everyone away. But then I remembered that Luke had had plenty of sandwiches to choose from before that. Maybe it was time to start paying attention to the newspapers, the way Eva did every morning at breakfast. She recycled them so fast, though, I doubt I could find one. But I knew one place that kept everything.

"Mom," I said, "can I go to the library? I could get you some new books."

"Sure." She handed me her just-finished one, along with the others she'd finished this week. "There's not much going on here."

AS I BIKED toward town, along the lake's edge, I thought about how nice libraries were for quiet days, days when I didn't feel like talking to anybody. Ms. Flynn, the librarian, didn't count: she was sensitive to moods and prone to silence.

"Hello, June," she said when she saw me. I plopped the return books on the counter. She grinned. "I see your mom went through her last bunch."

I nodded.

"How is she doing? How are you doing?"

"Do you keep old newspapers?"

"It's all online," Ms. Flynn said. She showed me how to get to the *Burlington Free Press* archive web page, and left me alone.

Where to begin? I typed "gay marriage" in the search box. Some editorials popped up. Not good. I needed facts, not opinions. I tried again, typing "civil union."

There it was. *Baker v. State*. After a lawsuit, the court ordered the legislature to address the couple's desire to marry. I read around the legal words. The House passed a bill for civil unions on March 17, 2000, then the Senate passed it, and Governor Howard Dean signed the bill into law on April 26. Right around the last softball game of sixth grade.

I clicked on letters to the editor after April 26. The anger could almost be heard out loud. Sometimes the letter writers used words I didn't understand, but I knew what they meant. They said that homosexuality was an "abomination" and that AIDS would spread. Some people tolerated gay people living together, but once they wanted to get married and raise children, that was where the letter writers drew the line. I scrolled down to read one letter writer who said that most gays were "pedophiles" and couldn't be trusted around innocent children. My heart sank. I was one of those kids.

"I've got some flyers to post; where can I put them?" Something familiar about the woman's tone made me look up. Lauren's mom was holding a mass of papers and pins in her hand.

"The public bulletin board is right over there," Ms. Flynn said. Then she glanced at the notice. "Oh, I'm afraid we can't post that in the library."

"Why not?"

"The bulletin board is reserved for announcements about meetings or events."

"That's ridiculous," Lauren's mother huffed. "This is important."

"I'm sorry—those are the rules."

She leaned into Ms. Flynn. "You're not changing them on me, are you? Don't tell me you're one of those gay lovers."

My hands went cold. I moved behind the monitor, hiding my face.

"Because we're taking back Vermont, you know. No hordes of homos moving in."

"I can't allow that kind of notice posted," Ms. Flynn said. I peeked around the computer. A red flush was creeping up her neck.

"Well, you can't stop me from handing out flyers. This is a free country."

"Yes, I think that's the point of the civil union law," Ms. Flynn replied. "All can live as they choose, even if you don't approve."

"Homosexuality is unnatural, especially in the eyes of God," she said, raising her voice.

"That's right," someone from behind the bestsellers rack said.

"I'm going to have to ask you to be quiet," Ms. Flynn said. "This is a library."

"Then I'll pass out my information outside," Lauren's mother said. No one else spoke as she humphed out the door.

I sank low, as if the word "homosexuality" had stuck

to my shirt. I hit "home," zapping the *Free Press* site I'd been reading.

Someone had left a book on the table next to me. I picked it up and flipped pages.

Ms. Flynn came over. "Did you find what you were looking for?"

I dropped the book and pushed in my chair. "Yes, thank you."

"It's good to see you — I'm glad you have time to read in the summer," she said. "Are you still making pies?"

I nodded. "I was thinking about entering the fair," I muttered. That didn't seem likely anymore; especially now that it looked like Mom was right about lying low.

"What a great idea! I have some exhibitor handbooks and forms right here. Take one, won't you?"

I zipped it into my backpack quickly.

"And here's a book for your mom," she said. "She's going to like it. Tell her to call me, OK, June?"

I pushed open the door, and stopped. A group was gathered around Lauren's mother. They were standing near the bike rack. Great.

"I can't believe the librarian wouldn't let you post this flyer," a man was saying. "A library is for information, isn't it?"

"Some people don't know what's right," Lauren's mother said. "Everybody is against gay marriage."

Head down, I knelt to unlock my bike, but someone shoved a flyer at me. "Take this home to your mom and dad, dear," she said. "We need everyone's support."

There, under the black letters, "Take Back Vermont," it said, "Boycott Gay Businesses." It named one of our favorite restaurants downtown and then, below that, "Stillwater Marina."

I grabbed at the flyer and stood up, shaking. I wanted to take them all and burn them. I wanted to shout, *That's not fair! What did we do to you?*

"Oh, June, it's you." Lauren's mother's tone changed.

"Hey, aren't you the girl that works at the marina?" The man stared at me. "She doesn't have a father," he announced to the crowd. "Her mother is gay."

I froze.

"Poor kid," someone said. "It's just wrong."

An older man agreed. "Queers shouldn't have children."

"If we don't stop them, homosexuals are going to ruin our state."

Lauren's mother looked me in the eye. "I hope your mother has told you about the dangers of her lifestyle," she said. "She and Eva could get AIDS! And then you'd be alone."

"They don't have AIDS," I said. "They are just regular people," I stammered in to the silence. Everyone stared at me, disapprovingly. I grabbed my bike. "They're just regular people."

I pedaled crazily, ferociously, away from the hateful crowd. *I'm just a kid with a mom who happens to be gay.* And then I wished she wasn't. And with that thought, I began to cry, and the wind slid my tears backwards, eddying in my ears.

chapter eight

"QUEERS SHOULDN'T HAVE children" echoed in my head as soon as I awoke. Images of the boycott flyer and the crowd scene pressed against my closed eyes. I couldn't tell Mom. If she knew that one of the people had been Lauren's mom, she'd tell Eva, and then Eva would make a scene. No one would know about Mom, I thought, if it wasn't for Eva.

I looked out my window and my mood eased. It was a glass day — that mystical once-in-a-while flat-lake time, perfect for reflection. It was so flat, it looked like you could walk on it, like in winter — though the frozen lake is a different place altogether. You can walk and walk until the horizon disappears in snow and clouds. A flat lake is the opposite — you can see above and below.

I knew just what to do. I climbed downstairs as quietly as I could, grabbed a bag of stale bread and a muffin.

"Where are you going?" Mom stood in the doorway, still in her pajamas.

"To feed the seagulls." I reached for the door. I wanted to be alone, on the water.

"Wait," she said, and then hesitated. "Thanks for going to the library for me."

I stared, wondering if she knew what had happened. But her next words made it clear she had no idea.

"I'm sorry for yelling at you about the burned pies."

"It's OK." I checked outside to see if the lake was still calm.

Mom put a hand on my shoulder. "Eva and I were talking. In case you were worried, all this backlash doesn't change our commitment to each other. The ceremony will be August third."

"What happened to lying low?" I blurted. "Why do I have to if you aren't?"

Mom smiled tightly. "I know you are mad about the pie contest," she said, "but that puts you in the spotlight. Eva and I are adults, and it's important for us to go forward. We can't let politics stand in the way of personal happiness. But you are just a kid, June, and I want you to stay out of it."

"That's impossible!" I jerked angrily away from her. As if I could avoid the hatred for Mom and Eva, and for everything they stood for—what was I supposed to do, never go to the marina shop, the library, the farm stand?

"I know it's hard — "

"If you're getting married, then I'm entering the fair. I'm not a baby." I slammed the door.

"Listen to me!" Mom called after me. "No pie contest!"

I raced down to the dock but stopped short. There, sitting on the edge, was Eva. The last person I wanted to see. Her back was hunched, her feet in the water. I walked silently over to the canoe and turned it over.

The noise made Eva turn. "Hi, June." She paused. "Out for a paddle?"

I nodded, lifting the bag of stale bread. I couldn't trust myself to speak.

She looked up at the sky and then back at me. "Can I come?"

"Since when do you like boats?" I snapped.

Her eyes dropped, and I regretted my quick words. I leaned on the oar and looked at the still lake. Eva and Mom were getting married. Could I get along with Eva? The right thing to do, I knew, was to say yes.

I threw in a second oar. "We have to be quiet," I said, pulling the canoe along the dock.

"Of course," Eva said. She got in, the wrong way, so I had to shift my weight to keep the canoe from tipping. She picked up the paddle and I set the pace, fast and steady.

With every stroke, I felt calmer and stronger. I steered the boat around the moorings. *This I can do,* I thought, and watched Eva's oar dip in and out, keeping the rhythm.

The canoe cut through the glass lake. From the back, I steered north, away from Luke's island — silently moving beyond Stillwater Cove.

The water was so clear, I could see clam trails breaking the sandy ridges on the lake bottom. I slowed down and listened to the water drip from the end of the paddle. Neither of us spoke.

A seagull soared overhead. I reached for the bread and let the canoe drift. I handed a slice to Eva. We tossed little pieces in, waiting for the birds to come. And slowly they did.

Eva threw one piece close to the canoe, and two males reached it at the same time, squawking.

"What a noisy crowd of birds," she said.

"I don't like crowds," I said. My mind flicked to that angry mob outside the library.

"I like dancing in a crowd, but I don't like a crowd of people in the waiting room, all needing attention," Eva said. She trailed her hand in the water and looked back at me. I purposefully stared into the water. At first I saw the sandy bottom, counting clams out of habit, and then I let my eyes shift until I saw my reflection. My eyes were so serious, and I saw a grown-up woman looking back at me. *Mom is wrong,* I thought defiantly. And then, the black, angry letters of the boycott flyer ruined my glass-lake morning. The hateful words replayed in my head — *"unnatural, queer, wrong"* — louder than the seagulls.

I looked at Eva, ripping the bread into small pieces. Her hair was short, the way people expected a lesbian to look.

I threw a piece of bread, hard. It was a good throw — far away from the canoe. Several seagulls dove for it.

"Are you getting along with Tina now?" Eva asked.

I watched the ripples from the canoe roll away. "Yeah."

"June."

I looked up. Eva's eyes were serious. "I'm sorry I lost my temper that day at the softball game."

"That's nothing compared to what's going on now," I said.

She raised her eyebrows. "Your mom and I are committed to each other."

"I'm not talking about the wedding or your fight." I threw the last chunk of bread in, too big for the birds. Slowly the gulls left, leaving only one swimming nearby, waiting to see if we had anything left to throw.

"Do you mean the sign?"

"You wouldn't understand."

"Try me." She leaned closer. The canoe tipped, and I shifted to counteract her move.

"Be careful!"

Eva gripped either side of the boat. "I wish you would talk to me, June, about boats, about your friends."

I wished she'd turn around again and start paddling. "You don't get it. You don't have kids."

Eva didn't move. "I'd like . . . Soon you'll be my stepdaughter."

"Great. Like I'll go around telling everyone I have two moms!" I grabbed the paddle and started for shore.

"June, I love—"

"You know what? You are the whole problem," I shouted. "Before you moved in, everything was fine. Queers aren't supposed to have kids anyway!"

Eva turned white. "How dare you—how dare you say—"

"That's what everybody says! What am I supposed to think?" I splashed my oar in again and again, breaking the surface with each violent stroke, recklessly spraying water everywhere. First Mom, now Eva. I wanted to get out, to get back to land. And then I knew what to do.

I jumped overboard.

"June!"

"I'm swimming back," I said. "You'll have to paddle back yourself." I launched into my strongest freestyle stroke, kicking up a fountain of water. *Who cares if she can't J stroke,* I thought. *I hope it takes her hours.*

chapter nine

IT TOOK HER thirty minutes to get back. She didn't say anything to Mom, so I didn't, either. Every now and then I'd catch Eva staring at me hard. I stayed out of the way, not talking to anybody. The problem with not talking, though, is that after a while you get so full of words, they could tumble out at any minute.

As soon as the sun rose the next morning, I whacked on my weather radio until the familiar announcer's voice rumbled: "Cloudy, clearing in the afternoon. South wind, ten to twelve knots. Lake temperature, sixty-eight degrees."

A good sailing day. I placed the red lens over my flashlight and faced it toward Luke's island. I needed help.

Mom and I had made cookies last night. It had been soothing to beat the batter and fill the cookie sheets. Baking together was her way of making peace, but I still couldn't talk to her. Unspoken worries weighed me down, like too much salt in the dough.

I wanted to tell Luke everything — about my fight with Mom, with Eva, and the library crowd — but I didn't know where to begin. I could at least show him the flyer. The marina could be in a lot of trouble with these posted around. And I had to tell him about Mom refusing to let me enter the pie contest.

It wasn't fair. Secretly, I had found the baked goods competition for children ages eight to twelve in the fair exhibitor handbook that Ms. Flynn had given me. The form was straightforward enough, but right at the top it said MOTHER'S NAME, FATHER'S NAME and, at the last line, SIGNATURE REQUIRED. I needed Luke to help me find a way around that.

"June!" Eva called up the loft stairs. "Luke is here!"

Perfect. Our light system worked. I pulled on my bathing suit and shorts. I tucked the fair form in my back pocket along with the flyer.

"Hey, June." Luke was in his bathing suit, ready for anything.

I gave him a "please wait" look, hoping he wouldn't ask what the trouble was in front of Eva.

But she didn't look up. She kept reading the newspaper.

"We're going sailing," I said.

"OK," she said without a glance.

I hesitated. "Do you think Mom needs help?"

"MJ is fine."

She probably can handle everything because there's no business, I thought as I glanced at the cove. One boat was gassing up, and I saw that Mom had put up a sign: FRESH COOKIES TODAY. I hoped someone—anyone—would come in.

Luke raced to the dock, and I followed. We quickly raised the mast and put in the rudder. "Where to, Captain?" Luke asked.

"Out," I said. We navigated through the moorings. Once we got beyond Luke's island, the wind picked up, and we pulled the sail in tight and hung out as far as we could. I let my hand trail in the water as I held on to the main sheet. I felt bad about Eva. I deserved the silent treatment, I guess. Maybe I'd been too hard on Mom, too.

When we reached the middle of the bay, Luke came about and ran before the wind. We were going fast, but the boom was off to the side, and we could sit on either side of the boat.

Luke turned to me. "Well?"

I stalled, checking the telltale on the stay to see if the sail was right. "Mom won't let me enter a pie in the fair," I said. "And I burned the pies the other night. I forgot to cover the edges."

"So? Everybody makes mistakes," Luke said.

"They're afraid of me being in the spotlight—"

"If you win . . . You might not," he teased.

"I'm a champion pie maker!" I boasted, then paused. "Somebody said gays shouldn't have kids."

"MJ is your mom!"

Eva isn't, I thought. But I wasn't ready to talk about that yet. I took the fair form out of my pocket and showed it to him. "It also could be this—"

"What about it?"

"It asks for the father's name," I said.

"June." Luke shook the paper with his free hand. "Don't you think I've filled out a form like this? You leave it blank. Not everybody's got a mother and a father."

My face reddened. I was so absorbed in my own problems, I had forgotten about families like Luke's. But my worries were bubbling over.

"Mom still won't sign it. She's right to be worried." I unfolded the flyer. "Yesterday at the library I saw Lauren's mother passing these out."

He took the flyer. The words "Take Back Vermont" and "Boycott Gay Businesses" jumped out in big letters. He whistled. "Wow. That's pretty low."

"That's why so many sandwiches are left over at the shop."

"More for us," he joked, but I didn't laugh. He paused. "We could bike around town and rip down all the flyers."

"If we could find them all." I dragged my hand in the water, watching the wake, feeling a lump in my throat. I didn't want to talk about what happened at the library anymore. "Eva wants to marry Mom in a civil ceremony. They asked me to be the flower girl."

"Cool," he said, and pretended to fling flowers overboard as he hummed "Here Comes the Bride."

I splashed him. "Only if I can wear a bathing suit under my dress."

"Look at it this way—you're getting another parent." He adjusted the tiller slightly. "My mother just doesn't want to live with us."

The sail flapped, then filled with wind again. Sometimes when I went over to his house, washed dishes were stacked haphazardly next to a screwdriver. I'd help Luke put things away, because there are always plenty of chores when it's just two. That's the way my life had been, Mom and I making it up as we went along. Who needs more? Especially somebody as opinionated as Eva. But sometimes I caught Mom's warm eyes, taking in the three of us at the table together. Their fight had scared me; it sounded like the kind between Luke's mom and dad before she left.

"She visits me only once a year, you know." Luke pulled the main sheet in, changing tack. "I can see how she couldn't live with us, on the island without a phone, but I don't see why I couldn't live with her sometimes."

"Did you ever ask her?" The last time Luke's mom had visited, I had watched her emerge from her car with

Quebec license plates in a tailored suit all wrong for getting in a boat to an island.

"She said managing the hotel takes all her time."

"That stinks." I folded the papers into small squares and put them back in my pocket.

Luke shrugged and turned the boat abruptly into the wind, letting the sail luff. He took off his shirt. "Man overboard!"

I shed my shorts. "Here I come!"

We splashed at each other but kept an eye on the sail. Luke was careful to push the nose of the boat back into irons, so it didn't take off without us.

"Let's go to Tin Can Island," I said when we got back on, dripping.

"Aye, aye, Captain."

In a moment, we were cruising toward the rock outcrop near the mouth of the bay.

"Hey, June," Luke said as we got close. "Do you see what I see?"

"What?"

"Berries—and they look ripe!"

I guided the boat along the edge of the rock, and Luke jumped off to tie up. I lowered the sail and joined him. The island was covered in goldenrod and harebells, with cypress around its edge. We picked our way around the poison ivy, straight to the berries.

A small patch of black raspberries dangled in the light.

"I can't believe they're ripe," I said, eating one. It tasted like a piece of sunshine.

"We're lucky the birds haven't eaten them all." Luke began collecting them in his shirt.

"What are you doing?"

"Picking them for the best pie ever, of course. The one you are going to enter in the fair."

I cupped a berry in my hand and rolled it back and forth. If I won, people would come back to the shop — never mind who owned it. I could add a few strawberries to sweeten up the black raspberries. What if I used three types of berries? Strawberries from Costas', these raspberries, and blueberries from the cliff-jumping spot. I was already beginning to imagine the flavor, with a little cinnamon, when I remembered the form.

"What about the entry form?" I asked.

"You could sign your mom's name."

"Luke!" I punched him lightly. "I bet Mrs. Costa doesn't need her parent's signature."

Luke looked at me. "Do you have to admit your age in the adult category?"

I stared. "You mean just enter that division?"

"Why not?"

It was a perfect idea. "Then I don't have to tell Mom," I said. "It could just be me, June Farrell, pie maker!"

"As long as you give me credit as your champion berry finder," he said, passing me his shirt filled with berries.

I placed the berries in the hull and watched Luke untie the boat. I touched my back pocket, feeling the form and flyer. All I needed was a little courage to enter the Champlain Valley Fair pie competition.

chapter ten

AS SOON AS I got home, I packed the black raspberries in our fridge — I didn't want to freeze them, just preserve them so they could last. The fair was only a week away, and I had to be ready.

Mom must have thought I would be hungry. I found a note propped up against the milk: *Come down to the marina right away, love Mom.*

Whatever, I thought. There was no chance to register for the pie competition today anyway — Luke had to help his dad in the studio. As I approached the dock, I was surprised to see more boats than I'd seen in a long time.

The bell sounded as I opened the door, and Mom looked up, grinning.

"I'm glad you're here. It's been the strangest day," she said. "I have to run up and make another batch of cookies."

"We've run out?"

"And almost all the sandwiches, too," she said. "I even had an order from Joe's gallery in Burlington. Someone drove down. Said they'd heard so much about them."

That was strange. It was the exact opposite of last week, when no one had come. My mind flashed to the boycott flyer, but it didn't make sense. I looked sharply at Mom to see if she suspected anything. Instead, she seemed happier than I'd seen her in a long time. It made me feel better.

"I was going to eat a sandwich but—"

"Don't worry—I'll make you something," Mom said. "Let's save these last two for customers."

The door jingled, and Mom scooted out as someone came in. I settled on the stool and pulled a Stillwater Marina cap on my head.

"Can I help you?"

The man smiled. "Just looking."

Unlike our regular customers, he was wearing jeans and a collared shirt. He was dressed for a city job, not as if he'd come in from the water, all windblown or wet. He looked along the shelves at the line and oil, and he picked up a cotter pin, flipping it around, as if he'd never seen one.

"That's for a sailboat," I said. "Do you need one?"

"No, no." He shifted his gaze to the food on display. "Do you have any pies?"

I shook my head, sorry again that I'd ruined the last

four. "We'll have hot cookies in the next half hour."

He picked up a ham sandwich instead. "I just wanted to lend my support," he said.

He handed me a ten, and I gave him his change. I didn't say any more, but I had a weird feeling that he had seen the "Boycott Gay Businesses" flyer.

He left, and several more people came in, buying the last sandwich and Ben & Jerry's ice cream bars. None of the purchases was large, but everything was adding up. The cash register had more crumpled tens and twenties than I'd seen all summer. Something was going on. I knew I should be glad for Mom's sake, but it was making me nervous. Just then Mom returned, sliding me a peanut butter and jelly and waving freshly wrapped cookies.

"Chocolate chip," she said.

"Great," a woman gushed as she approached the counter. She held two postcards in her hand but had been browsing. She snatched up two pairs of cookies. "To share, in the office," she said.

Mom rang it up. "Five eighty-nine."

"Is that all?" The woman looked around the shop.

Mom laughed. "It's not often that I get a customer who wants to spend more."

"I want to be supportive, that's all." She picked up a Stillwater visor. "How much is this?"

"That's fifteen ninety-nine," I said.

"I'll take it."

Mom added the item in, her mind quietly working. "What did you mean, 'supportive'?"

"I think it's just terrible what's going on. I think everybody deserves to be happy, and it doesn't matter who owns a business."

I pulled my cap low down over my eyes. It felt like my tongue was stuck on the roof of my mouth like the peanut butter I'd just eaten. I suddenly hated this cheerful woman. I watched her leave.

"How unusual," Mom murmured.

"Luke and I found some black raspberries." I needed to change the subject.

"That will make a nice pie."

I nodded. I didn't mention the fair. I shifted in my stool. It was a good plan to register in the adult division; yet it made me uncomfortable not to tell the truth.

The door jingled, and we both looked up. A strong woman with deep lines on her face strode in, wearing a jaunty hat over her white curls.

"Ruth!"

I was surprised. Ruth played tennis with Eva occasionally, but she was better known as an opinionated letter writer to the local paper and a talker at town meetings. She probably had a position on the civil union law, but I didn't know it. I jumped off the stool and nervously realigned all the cotter pins in neat rows.

"MJ! Got any pies? No? What, didn't expect customers? I wouldn't think you would take this lying down. You and Eva are fighters, aren't you?"

"We've had a slow week, but nothing we can't handle——"

"Nonsense! Eva did the right thing——strike back! Gather your allies!"

Mom's bewildered expression flicked to me.

I ran up to the counter, placing myself between Mom and Ruth. "Try one of these chocolate chip cookies! They're fabulous!"

"Sure, honey. This must be tough on you. But you two have held your own all along. I'm not worried about you. What else should I buy?"

I grabbed a map of the lake. "Have you got the latest depth chart? You'll need this if you want to know the ins and outs of every cove."

"Sure, and sunscreen, too, for my next fishing venture——"

Mom clapped her hands on the counter. "Ruth. What are you talking about? June, what is going on?"

I looked at Ruth and then down at the floor.

Ruth cocked her hat back. "You haven't heard? The flyers are showing up all over town."

"What flyers?"

I felt in my back pocket. I was still wearing the same jeans. I pulled out the "Boycott Gay Businesses" flyer, unfolded it slowly and laid it flat on the counter. Ruth was already talking.

"This kind of thing is outrageous. I'm glad Eva sent out the e-mail, alerting everyone. You've got a lot of support, MJ, and there's no way we'd let one of our Vermonters suffer this kind of injustice. We're all behind you, MJ, so ring me up."

Mom closed her eyes. I came around and gave her a hug. "I didn't want you to worry. Please don't be sad."

"I'm OK. You don't need to worry about me." Her squeeze was quick, her eyes flashing to the flyer.

Ruth adjusted her hat and pulled out her purse. "So when are you and Eva tying the knot? Don't forget to invite me!"

Mom murmured, "August third," gave Ruth her change, and they said their goodbyes.

As soon as she was gone, Mom picked up the flyer and turned to me. "How long did you know about this? Why didn't you tell me?"

"I didn't want you to worry," I repeated.

"My June bug." Mom gave me an exasperated shake. "I'm the one in charge of the worrying!"

"No worries, right, Mom?" I tried to say it like she did, but it came out squawky like a seagull.

She tossed her cap on the counter and shook her head angrily. "I thought you were having a little bit of trouble with Tina, but this . . . If people are attacking my family, my business . . ." She seemed to see me again. "Can you handle the cash register? I need to call Eva. I cannot believe she did this without telling me."

Mom's anger didn't make sense. "But isn't it good to have all these customers again?"

"No! Yes, of course!" Mom grabbed her cell phone. "But it's not exactly lying low, this telling everyone our problems."

As I rang up another sale, I had to admit I was impressed with Eva. Telling people to shop at the targeted businesses was a good idea. It was better than Luke's idea to tear the flyers down. Maybe Eva and I could change people's minds. I would do my part, too.

I would make a champion pie for the fair.

chapter eleven

"IT'S HERE!"

I wiped cinnamon toast crumbs from my mouth. "What?"

"The fair, silly," Tina's voice over the phone filled the kitchen the next morning. "They're setting up. My dad said he saw the Ferris wheel on the fairgrounds when he drove by this morning. Let's go!"

"Now?" I glanced at Eva, but she was absorbed in the newspaper. I hoped it wasn't too late to register for the pie contest. I'd filled out the adult form last night, by flashlight. Luke was busy with his dad today; it would be nice to go with Tina.

"You're the only other kid I know who has entered the fair," she said. "I'll meet you at the stoplight in fifteen minutes, OK?"

We said goodbye, and I clanked my plate in the sink.

"I'm going biking with Tina," I said, and waited for Eva to give me the third degree — or at least remind me to put my plate in the dishwasher.

"I'll tell MJ." Her eyes didn't leave the page with the headline, "Candidate Denounces Civil Union Law."

I grabbed my sweater and paused at the door. Maybe it had been a mistake to give Eva the cold shoulder. She was turning out to be pretty good at it, too.

A "thank you" sat on my tongue, without budging. I was grateful to Eva for bringing customers to the marina, and I almost wanted to tell her my plan to help, too. But how do you talk to someone who won't look at you?

AS I BIKED down the road, I thought about how nice it was to see Mom busy again. I could tell she was still mad at Eva for not discussing it with her first. They had been up late talking. One e-mail wouldn't change everything, though. It was more important than ever for me to win the pie contest, for Mom and the shop.

Tina waved to me when I reached our meeting spot. "C'mon, let's go see what's set up. I can already smell the cotton candy."

Tina's pink nails gripped her handlebars as she rode high on a hand-me-down boy's bike. I wouldn't have minded it, but Tina always worked hard at looking like a girl. I guess it came from having two brothers.

At the fairgrounds, we stashed our bikes and walked through the exhibitors' entrance. Trucks and cars were parked in and around the booths, unloading.

The fair was at once exotic and ordinary. Men with faded snake tattoos connected wires, hoisted tents, and tied ropes. Women, cigarettes hanging from cracked lips, hauled equipment into place. I remembered the rides from last year, the funnel cakes, and tie-dyed shirts. Even the crocheted tablecloths and knitted baby outfits looked familiar. Except this time was my first pie competition.

We watched a large truck back up to position the Zipper, the upside-down ride.

"Will you try it this year?" Tina asked.

"I don't know. What about you?"

"Maybe."

We went over to the farm area and watched the men set up the corrals. Soon each pen would hold a prize pig, goat, or cow.

"Moonbeam's doing great," Tina said. "My dad and I will bring her down tomorrow."

I hadn't seen Mr. Costa since I'd overheard him at the farm. But he was helping Tina get ready for the fair. It was weird the way people could be good and bad. My form bulged in my back pocket, making me anxious.

Tina saw me kicking the hay. "Do you want to go look at the culinary section?"

I took a deep breath. "My mom doesn't want me to register for the fair."

"What?! I thought you already had. That's awful." Tina grabbed my arm. "Let's go see if it's not too late."

I hesitated. "I'm going to enter the adult berry pie competition."

"Why?"

"This way, I don't need anybody's signature." I glanced at her, hoping I didn't need to explain more.

But Tina got it. "That means you'll be competing against my mom."

I nodded. I had worried about going for the adult contest for two reasons: it would make it harder to win, and it might make Tina mad. But I didn't have any other choice. "Is that OK?"

"I guess," she said. "But you can't just walk into the office and ask for an adult form."

I unfolded the piece of paper from my back pocket. "I got this from the library."

She read it over. "It looks like you filled it out right."

We started walking toward the office door. My mouth was dry, and I got worried all over again. How could I do this? "Maybe you could turn it in, and say your mother asked you to drop it off."

"But what if it's someone who knows me? And my mother really has turned in her entry form."

I looked at the office door. If someone was going to lie, I figured it should be me.

"I'll do it," I said.

"I'll come."

I was surprised — and glad. "Thanks."

The woman behind the counter was stapling entry forms.

"Hi," I said, too quietly. I tried again louder. "My aunt was hoping it isn't too late to enter the berry pie competition." I pushed the form across the counter.

"She's just in time." The woman put on her glasses and read over my entry form. My breath came ragged, as if I had been running. I clenched my fingers, waiting.

Finally, she took out a pen and wrote a number on it. "Tell her she's Number forty-seven and to deliver her pie on Monday by ten a.m."

I nodded, relief steadying me. "Does that mean there are forty-seven pies entered in the contest?"

"That's right," she said. "So tell her good luck!"

As soon as the door shut behind us, Tina and I grinned.

"The competition will be much harder now, you know," Tina said.

"Number forty-seven can handle it!" I did a cartwheel right there in the dirt. I was registered!

Tina clapped and laughed. When I came up right side up again, I was face-to-face with Mr. Costa, stopping his farm truck beside us.

"Well, look who's here."

"It's Tina and that test-tube kid!" Sam jeered from the flatbed.

"No name-calling, son," Mr. Costa said. He looked down at me from the driver's seat. My face was red from Sam's words.

Mr. Costa rested his arm on the window. "You're turning out fine, it seems, but I should tell you I don't approve of homosexuals like your mom raising kids and wanting to get married," he said. "And you're getting old enough to start thinking about boys. If you ever get mixed up, you can come on over to our place. You're always welcome."

I couldn't speak.

"Dad!" Tina said.

"June's normal — she's got a boyfriend," Sam teased. "Weren't you and Luke holding hands the other day?"

Tina squealed, "You never told me."

"He's not my boyfriend." My voice came out hot and fast.

"That's OK, sugar, you're a little young," Mr. Costa said. "Tina, Mom needs you back at the farm to watch Tim. He's underfoot. We've got some hay to deliver." And he drove off.

The dust from the truck filled my eyes, but the bumper

sticker on the back of the truck was unmistakable: TAKE BACK VERMONT.

"Can you believe my dad is talking to us about boys!" Tina laughed. "Tell me about Luke! What happened?"

"Nothing." I strode over to our bikes and grabbed my helmet, struggling with the strap.

"What's wrong?" she asked. "Why are you leaving?"

I picked up my bike. I was shaking all over. "It's just like at the game at school," I said. "You're on his side, aren't you?"

"What are you talking about? You aren't mad about what he said about your mom, are you? Just don't pay any attention. He was concerned, anyway."

I stared at her. "I can't believe you're saying that."

"What?"

"He's wrong, you know," I shouted. "My mom is a great parent, and she deserves to marry Eva if she wants. They can get married just like anybody else!"

I didn't wait for Tina to answer. I jumped on my bike and pedaled for home.

chapter twelve

I WOKE UP to the sound of a woodpecker tapping on the pine tree. I sat up and turned my binoculars to him. He was alone, as alone as I felt. I couldn't go through with the pie contest. Not if I had to deal with people making fun of my family all the time. I wondered what happened if someone didn't turn in a pie. I guessed the judges just assumed it was a no-show and threw the entry form away. That would be Number forty-seven.

I spotted the rowboat cutting across the cove, but it was Joe not Luke. Then I remembered Joe was going to handle the shop today — Mom and I were going to Burlington to buy a flower girl dress. I flopped back onto my bed, staring at the ceiling. No one was a flower girl at my age.

Mom knocked and poked her head in. "Let's go!"

I groaned.

"C'mon—I'm buying you clothes!"

"OK, but no pink."

Mom and Eva had soft smiles now whenever they talked about the wedding plans. Mom said she knew the people who mattered—Joe, Ms. Flynn the librarian, even Ruth—supported their right to get married if they wanted. I made an effort, but Eva and I were still not on the best of terms. I didn't know how to break the stand-off with her.

Once in the car, I glanced at the windshield. We hadn't had any notes or signs after that one time. It didn't surprise me. Whoever was behind it, maybe Lauren's mother or even Mr. Costa, had gotten organized and made all those flyers boycotting gay businesses. I began counting how many "Take Back Vermont" signs I saw compared to "Keep it Civil."

"We sent out the invitations," Mom said once we got on the highway for Burlington.

"Who's coming?" I had counted ten "Take Back Vermont" signs; six "Keep It Civil" signs.

"Well, so far, Joe and Luke have RSVP'd, and so has Anne Flynn."

Great. Three people. I spotted another "Take Back" sign, making the score eleven to six.

"No worries, right, June?" Mom said.

"No worries," I said. It was the old game, but I wasn't playing truthfully. I was worried about everything: Tina, the wedding, my no-show pie. On top of everything, I didn't know what to do about Eva. The silence was making me miserable.

At the department store, I trailed behind Mom, fingering various dresses. Nothing seemed right.

"I'm wearing my lilac dress," she said. "And Eva is wearing a red dress—well maybe more of a burgundy wine color. We thought you'd look great in something, hmm, green."

I looked around. I hoped no one had heard. "Blue," I said defiantly.

A saleswoman approached. "May I help you?"

"Yes," Mom said. "We're looking for an elegant dress for a special occasion for my daughter."

"How nice," she said. "Should we head to the teen section?"

I felt like the woman was looking right at my chest. "I'm twelve," I said.

"Growing up so fast," Mom murmured, mussing my hair. I was about to scream.

"What's the special occasion?"

I gave Mom a look, but she went ahead and said, "A wedding."

"Oh, how lovely! Who is getting married?"

"I am," Mom said, then gave me a reassuring squeeze.

I was glad she didn't say any more. Not every conversation had to be a political act, did it?

The saleswoman pulled a couple of dresses off the rack in pinks, lavenders, and purples.

I folded my arms. "I like blue," I said.

"Well, here's a nice one." She pulled down a lake blue dress, with navy trim. It was short-sleeved, with a wide skirt. "It has little flowers around the neckline."

"June, they look like blueberry flowers," Mom exclaimed.

Even I had to admit it was perfect. I tried on several others, including a green one, but the blueberry dress was the one.

Mom put her hands on my shoulders. We both straightened as we gazed in the mirror. My head had reached Mom's shoulder—and my hair was not in a ponytail for once. I wasn't flower girl material anymore.

"June, you look beautiful." Mom touched my hair lightly, and for once I didn't mind.

With the blueberry dress folded in a bag, we stopped in a few more stores. Mom found new shoes for herself and white sandals for me.

"Let's get ice cream to celebrate," Mom said, pushing open the door at Ben & Jerry's. "I never take clothes shopping for granted with you."

I ordered my favorite, chocolate chip cookie dough. Mom had hers, rainforest crunch. Eva wouldn't approve —she wanted us to try new flavors.

"Eva and I thought you could hold a bouquet of

Queen Anne's lace," Mom said, as we settled into a booth.

I licked off a piece of dough. "Don't you think I'm too old to be a flower girl?"

"What would you like to be?"

"The maid of honor."

Mom wrapped her napkin around her cone. "Usually, the maid of honor is the bride's best friend."

I grinned. "That's me, isn't it?"

She smiled. "There's nothing conventional about this wedding, so why not?"

"Yes!"

"I'll tell Eva," Mom said, then added, "We know this wedding hasn't been on your list of favorite things to do this summer."

Somehow, it didn't seem like the worst thing anymore. "You changed your mind about the wedding, about being in the spotlight."

"I've never changed my mind about Eva, but I was worried about you." She pushed her glasses back. "I was trying to protect you—that's what moms do. But you've been tackling prejudice all along, and that's not going to change."

I dragged my tongue over the top of the cone. It was fine for her, but now lying low seemed like the right thing for me. I no longer wanted to be Tina's friend or enter my pie in the fair.

Mom continued. "And getting married makes sure we're treated like any other family, even if some people don't see it that way."

"Like the eleven people with 'Take Back Vermont' signs," I pointed out.

"What about the 'Keep It Civil' signs?"

"Only six." I licked my ice cream. I wanted to tell her about the day at the library, but the words stuck in my throat like cookie dough. Or what had happened with Mr. Costa and Tina, but that reminded me how Sam had called Luke my boyfriend.

"Can I ask you something else?" I said. "About boys."

Mom's cone stopped inches from her lips. "What about them?"

"Do you think . . ." I hesitated. "I mean, you may not know, but do you think I will be like you?"

"Oh, honey," she said. "Only you will know. Deep down, I think you might know already."

My stomach quivered, remembering when Luke had held my hand the day on the cliff and on the dock. I wondered if Tina had ever held a boy's hand, not counting Tim's.

"Hey, you two." Eva appeared. "I thought I might find you here."

I stiffened. What was she doing here? This was my time with Mom.

Mom gave her a hug. I looked away, hoping no one

noticed. "We were just talking about the wedding." Mom winked at me.

"What, same old flavor?" Eva teased. She was wearing her hospital coat.

"Were you trying to track us down?" I asked.

"June!"

"I won't bother you two for long—I'm taking a little break."

I balled up my napkin. "I'm going to be the maid of honor," I announced.

Eva was surprised. She looked at me and then at Mom. "Is that what you want?"

"It's what we both decided," Mom said. Now it was Eva's turn to feel left out. I was glad.

Eva and Mom began to discuss details about the caterer. I finished my cone, hoping no one was listening to them. I excused myself and headed to the restroom.

Just as I shut a stall door, some girls all talking at once came in. With a start, I recognized Tina's voice. I looked through the crack: She was with Lauren and Kelly. I hadn't seen them since school had ended.

My face burned. I couldn't believe she was with them. Any hope that Tina understood how mean they had been that day at the softball game disappeared. She obviously didn't get it. She was from a regular American apple pie family: Mom, Dad, two boys, and a girl. I couldn't stand it. A friend wouldn't laugh off an insult. Luke wouldn't have laughed.

I didn't make a sound. If I walked out, I'd have to decide whether or not to ignore them. My skin prickled. I wondered if they would ignore *me*.

"Wasn't that guy cute?" Kelly squealed.

"No way," Lauren said. "He was so gay!"

Anger kick-started inside me. Tina wouldn't tell Lauren to stop saying "gay." It was all the same — at the game, with her family or her friends. Tina didn't get it, and, what's more, she didn't have the guts to stand up to any of them.

I banged open the door just in time to see Tina cover her smile with her pink nails. Our eyes met. She looked away first. I didn't say a word and walked out.

To my horror, I saw that Mom and Eva were holding hands. Out of the corner of my eye, I saw Tina, Lauren, and Kelly heading to the counter to order.

"Let's go," I said, blocking any view of the table.

"I guess I'm ready," Mom said.

Eva pitched the napkins on our way out. "Hey, isn't that Tina over there?"

I turned toward the door. "Don't you have to go back to work?"

"June, that's enough," Mom said.

"I do have to go." Eva gave Mom a kiss. "Bye, June."

I kept on walking.

chapter thirteen

THE NEXT DAY it was raining, and Luke's signal was yellow. In a way I was glad—I still hadn't talked to him since Sam had called him my boyfriend. Nothing had changed as far as Luke knew, of course—it was me I was worried about. It seemed like I had lost all my friends in one stroke. The only constant was the lake, and even she seemed to be blue today. Every worry, every insult baked inside of me.

The blueberry dress hung ghostly on the closet door; I turned my back to it as I pulled on shorts and a T-shirt.

Downstairs, the kitchen still smelled of pies; Mom and I had made four berry pies after shopping—the silver lining of yesterday. I ate breakfast in silence, idly skimming the comics. Mom and Eva didn't seem to notice. They were talking quietly—Eva said something about her father having e-mailed to say he wouldn't come. She looked sad, and Mom gently rested her hand on Eva's. I turned back to the comics. If Eva's own father wouldn't come to the wedding, how could we be sure anyone would?

"June, can you work the shop today?" Mom asked. "A photographer is coming."

"For what?"

"For the wedding, honey." Mom glanced at Eva, who sighed and straightened her dress.

So you're really going to go through with it, I wanted to say. The wedding worried me. It seemed crazy to act like everything was going to be fine when so many people thought it was wrong. And I still hadn't figured out how to be around Eva.

Not talking turned out to be easy. Business was slow although a little better since Eva's e-mail. But even that rush of friends had eased. I swatted at flies, tidied up the stack of Lake Champlain maps, and spun around on the stool.

"Got any special pies?"

It was Ms. Flynn, the librarian. I was so surprised, I jumped off my stool. "What are you doing here?"

Ms. Flynn laughed. "I don't live at the library, June. I've got a good friend coming over to dinner, and I want to serve the best Vermont has to offer."

I smiled for the first time all day. "I made this straw-berry-blueberry," I said. "But I used store-bought blue-berries."

"It will be fabulous," she said. "MJ and Eva must be very proud of your baking talent."

"Thanks," I said, and felt better. I noticed, too, how comfortable she was mentioning two moms. I wished everyone felt that easy about it. Including me.

"That's ten sixty-nine," I said. "Do you want anything else?"

"No, thanks." She handed me her money. "Pies like this shouldn't be kept a secret—did you enter the fair?"

I nodded. I didn't mention my plan to let entry Number forty-seven be a no-show.

"I'm glad." She paused at the door. "I was worried that that woman with her anti-gay flyers upset you."

"Not really." I tried to say it casually, but my face grew hot.

"When things like that happen, I'm always disappoint-ed. But I never quit."

"Quit what?"

"Standing up for what's right," she said, looking out at the rain falling on the lake. "It takes courage to stand up for your beliefs."

Maybe Tina was afraid to speak up. It was hard, I knew that. It was hard even for me to tell Tina that she was wrong. Or for me to tell Eva how I felt about the wedding or her (if I even knew). Or to tell Ms. Flynn that I planned to drop out of the contest.

Ms. Flynn continued. "My friend Alice Walker once wrote that the other choice, the choice not to act and to miss the chance to experience other people at their best, never appealed to her." She turned to look at me. "It doesn't appeal to me, either. And I bet it doesn't to you, either, June."

"What do you mean?"

"Well, you've registered for the pie contest in the fair. That's one way to stand up for yourself." She opened her umbrella. "That's letting the world know who you are despite how other people define you."

I stared. "You mean, as a girl with two moms or a champion pie maker?"

"Which would you prefer?" she asked. "Think about it."

As I watched Ms. Flynn leave, my thoughts bubbled up like a finished pie. I *was* brave—I had stood up to Tina, to Sam, and even to Lauren's mother. They were all wrong, all of them, and Mr. Costa, and even the mystery person who had hammered in that first sign. And Mom wanted to marry Eva. She was standing up for herself. We had to keep living our lives, and for me, that meant making pies, the best pies. Even if Mom didn't know I had entered the Champlain Valley Fair pie competition, I had to make the right choice for me.

I was going to do it. I had the makings of a champion pie with the lucky berries from Tin Can Island. I needed only two cups of blueberries, and I knew exactly where the most special ones grew.

AFTER LUNCH, I grabbed a bowl and hiked up behind the old camp. The rain was light in the woods, and the trees dampened any sounds. The world seemed small, as if only I existed. The pine needles were soft and the cedars sheltering, like arms keeping me safe from the cliff's edge. A woodpecker hammered on a trunk, startling me.

Then I smelled sweetness. Or maybe just the sight of the ripe blueberries made my mouth water. They were perfect—a foggy blue that turned purple blue when touched. I couldn't believe my luck. I found a good spot to sit, where I could reach handfuls all around me. I began picking, stealing a few for my mouth.

I wished Luke were here. My stomach fluttered a little like when I stood on roller skates for the first time. I wondered if Luke felt anything for me. I wondered, too, if Tina agreed with what her dad told her about my parents. That hate was like a sour ingredient in a pie, and I wondered if you could get the taste out once it was added.

"Blueberries!"

I looked up. Little Tim Costa was sitting in my bushes.

"What are you doing here?"

"Me and Tina are picking berries," he said between swallows.

Tina was right behind him.

"Hi." I felt a sudden irrational anger — this was *my* secret spot, *my* special berries for my champion pie.

"There was nothing to do at the farm." She sat down and began to pick.

I ignored her. I didn't say anything, either about Tim getting a stomachache or muddy, which he was doing. I wasn't about to be friendly.

Tina wasn't her usual self, either. She worked quietly, sitting near but not too close. Maybe she would say she was sorry. Then I wondered if I should apologize for yelling — or leave.

After a long time, she spoke. "Did you decide what kind of pie to make?"

"Yes."

"More blueberries," Tim said, walking toward another bush.

"Don't go too far," she said. When he was out of earshot, she leaned over. "At the fair, after you left, Sam slipped on a cow patty."

I grinned. I couldn't help it.

"He deserved it," Tina said. "I don't care how you were born. He shouldn't have said that."

"What about Lauren and Kelly?" I blurted out.

"They don't mean anything by it."

I looked right at her. "I'm going to speak up next time. I'm going to do it for Mom and Eva."

Tina picked a few blueberries and put them in my bowl. "My mom's making the same old strawberry pie. I bet you'll win with these blueberries."

"Thanks," I said. Then I asked, "What do your parents really think of my mom and Eva?"

Tina looked down and rolled a berry around in her hand. "Mom is a good friend to M.J., even when my dad starts talking. And I like Eva."

"They're all I've got," I said.

The rain still fell, dappling the surface of the lake.

"I think it must be cool to be an only child," Tina said. "I'm sick of brothers." Suddenly we both looked up. "Tim?"

I scrambled to my feet. "I'll go this way; you go that way."

Tina called for Tim, her voice rising in fear. My own palms grew sweaty. Then we both heard a splash.

"June!" Tina pointed.

I looked down the cliff at large circles — too large to be the wake of a fish feeding.

"He can't swim! How do you get down?"

"There's only one way." I slid off my sneakers. I eased down to the lower shelf, remembering how just weeks ago the boys had egged me on. This time the silence from the lake screamed; Tim was taking too long to come up. Fears passed from my mind to my hands, which became as wet as if I were already in the water — what if I jumped on him? What if he pulled me under? What if I hit a rock?

Then I thought of Luke. I jumped without looking.

My breath was gone. I made no noise. I couldn't see. Then I hit hard and my shorts sheared up, and water burned in my nose. I came up for air, untangled my arms from my shirt, and shook my hair. Tim! I spotted him. He had found the surface, thrashing. I was glad he wasn't sinking, but when I touched him, he pulled on me and we both went under. I kicked and kicked with all my might.

"Tim, it's June — stop — " My mouth filled with water, and I struggled free of him to cough and catch my breath.

His frightened eyes fixed on me, and I reached for him again.

"It's me," I said. I locked my arm around his shoulders and head. The right position returned from some far-off pocket of my mind; a swim instructor had once shown me a rescue hold. Tim still struggled but began to relax.

Treading water, I turned to the cliff. We had drifted out far. I couldn't see Tina — where was she? It would be a long swim, and then what? Tim was too small to climb the cliff. But I had to reach the edge, at least to rest.

I kicked my legs, scissorlike, trying a sidestroke with

Tim's awkward bulk across my body. My mouth kept filling with water, though I wasn't sure if it was lake or rain. I gasped and struggled for a rhythm. As the cliff neared, I looked left and right, hoping to find a ledge, a place where I could pull Tim up. He was crying steadily now. The cliffs seemed sheer, like a fortress — where was the path Luke had used? Where was Tina? I began to panic, when my leg banged against something. A rock! I pulled my knees up and planted my feet firmly on the submerged rock.

"Tim, we're OK now." I tried to show him how he could stand up, but he clung tighter to me, crying harder. I made some soothing sounds until I could no longer think of anything to say. *We're both alive,* I reminded myself. I held on to him, my arms aching, while he cried. I don't know when he stopped or when we stopped shivering. I stood like a heron, waiting, cold.

And then I heard the unmistakable sound of a motor.

"June!"

It was Eva and Luke. I had never been so happy to see them.

In a moment, Eva had pulled Tim from me, stripped his clothes off, and wrapped him in a blanket. Luke helped me on board, throwing a sweatshirt my way before gunning the motor.

"Tina used your light to signal to me," he said. "She

told me you jumped off the cliff." He gave me a smile. "Not so hard, right?"

"Right." I began to shiver again.

"Put on the sweatshirt," Eva said, fussing over me. I struggled to put my arm through, and she pulled on the sleeve and drew me in for a quick hug. "You did a brave thing." My insides began to thaw.

● ● ●

BACK AT THE marina, Mom grabbed the bow of the boat, and Tina sobbed as Eva carried Tim to shore.

"I ran all the way to your house—I was so afraid—" Tina gasped, and pulled Tim in for a hug.

"That was the right thing to do," Eva said. "He's OK. June saved him."

"Oh, June," Mom said as she wrapped a towel around me. She kept her arms around me in the warmest hug. In a moment Eva joined us. I looked up at her. "Thanks," I whispered.

"I've been working on my boating skills," Eva admitted.

I glanced at Mom as I answered Eva. "You don't have to love boats like Mom and I do."

"How else can I be a part of this family?" Eva said, then added in her doctor voice, "Let's get these two by the wood stove. Your mom started it."

JENNIFER GENNARI

Inside was the best kind of warm, not just stove-warm but people-warm.

"June thought she was too chicken to jump, but I knew she could," Luke said.

"I don't think I could ever do it again," I said, but as the words came out, I knew it wasn't true.

Just then, the Costas arrived. Their eyes went straight to Tim, who was wearing a Stillwater Marina T-shirt and drying by the stove.

"Timmy!" Mrs. Costa hugged him tight. Mr. Costa put his arm around both his wife and son. "No more cliff hikes for you, young man," he said, and brushed Tim's wet hair off his forehead.

"I slipped." Tim started to cry again. "June jumped in to get me."

"You're a brave girl," Mr. Costa said to me. "Thank you."

"It was Tina's quick thinking, too, to signal Luke," Mom said. "You have a fine daughter."

"As do you," Mrs. Costa said.

"Won't you stay for a coffee? And I think we have some pie, too," Eva said.

A silence stretched—and stretched. It was as if my red lens-covered flashlight had flickered on and beamed the word LESBIANS above our heads, filling that silence. Mr. Costa stepped right into it, firm. "I think we'll just get Tim home. He's dry now."

"Thank you for the kind offer," Mrs. Costa said as she picked up Tim.

I felt like a statue, but Tina nearly knocked me over with a hug. "I was so scared," she whispered. "Thank you for saving my brother."

I held her tight.

"See you at the fair," she said. "Good luck with your pie."

"You entered the pie contest?" Mom and Eva said together.

I nodded. I looked from one to the other. "I didn't want to give up."

"I'm glad you didn't," Eva said.

"That's what I was doing on the cliff," I said. "I was collecting those blueberries you found for me, Luke. I want to make a blueberry-strawberry–black raspberry pie."

"I'll go back and get them," he said.

"I'll bring strawberries over tomorrow," Tina said.

Luke cheered. "This is going to be the best pie!"

chapter fourteen

THE MORNING OF opening day of the Champlain Valley Fair was hot and sunny. I had spent the day before making my pie with wild blueberries, strawberries, and the black raspberries. Mom had watched me, but I did it all by myself. I carefully wrote down everything that I put in, including the pinch of cinnamon, and named it "Wild Berry Pie." The crust was just right—and I didn't burn it.

"June, you ready?" Mom called. "Luke's already here!"

I scrambled to get on my clothes. All the pie entries had to be turned in by ten a.m. The judges would make their decision by three p.m.

Cars were already lined up at the fairgrounds gate. Music, voices, and farm sounds intermingled with the smells of funnel cake, cotton candy, and barbecue. People crowded the ticket booth, and Luke and I surged ahead to the gate.

"Look, there's a huge sand castle!" Luke shouted.

Plastic figurines jousted on the drawbridge, and a flag flew from the top of the turreted castle.

"See that — there's even a dragon in the moat!"

"We can look more later," Eva said. "Let's go to the culinary hall and drop this pie off."

The culinary hall overflowed with smells and sights — giant pumpkins and sunflowers, perfect roses in pencil-thin vases, and tomatoes of every variety. Baked breads and a whole section of muffins stood in neat rows. A few had ribbons — blue for first, red for second, yellow for third, and white for honorable mention. I squeezed Mom's hand then, and tried to imagine a blue ribbon on my pie.

A long table was lined with a sea of pies already. As Mom handed over my creation, I felt like it was swallowed up. Would Number forty-seven stand out from all the rest?

Mom and Eva insisted on riding the merry-go-round next, even though Luke and I complained we were too old. But somehow bobbing up and down on the paint-chipped horses together was the perfect way to start the day.

"We're off to the arts and crafts," Mom said. "We'll meet back at the hall at three, OK?"

Luke and I went through the haunted house and on

every fast, spinning ride we saw. We played the arcade games until Luke shot down enough balloons to win a bear. "For you," he said. My insides jumped in a much nicer way than when I had gone off the cliff.

"Let's get our picture taken," Luke said. In the photo booth, we sat side by side, with the bear in my lap. Luke pulled on his ears and I laughed; when we looked at the five pictures, Luke was silly in every one. In last year's photos, I remembered, Tina had been with us.

"Let's go see if Moonbeam won," I said.

The farmyard section was like a different world within the fair. Funnel cake fumes were replaced with the scent of hay mixed with the manure of so many animals — goats, chickens, rabbits, and, of course, cows.

"Hey, Luke and June!" Tina was waving her hands by Moonbeam's stall. "I won second place!"

We high-fived, and I gazed at Moonbeam's glistening sides. "You must have been here early, brushing her."

"Yeah, my dad and I got here at seven a.m.," she said. "Mom's keeping Tim on a short leash, too, over by the 4-H booth."

I went over and gave Tim another hug. "Next time you go swimming, wear a life jacket, OK?"

Just then, Sam came up. "I'm done spreading the hay. Can I go now?"

"Where are your manners? Say hello to June," Mrs. Costa said.

"Hey, June," he said. I waited for him to say something low.

Instead, Mrs. Costa came around the table and squeezed me hard. "You're one special girl. I know your mom is raising you right."

"Thank you," I said.

"And she sure taught you how to make pie," she said.

"Did you win?" Tina asked.

Mrs. Costa looked at her watch. "It's time to go see."

LUKE, TINA, AND I ran, dodging people, past the trac- tors, booths of tie dye and Indian jewelry, and Ben & Jerry's ice cream. We ran into the culinary hall.

Mom and Eva almost collided with us.

"There you are!" Mom grabbed my hand. "They're about to announce the winners of the adult division. Kids will be next."

"Let's go," Eva said. She reached for my other hand. Our grasp was unsure at first, but her hand was warm and steady.

The main room was crammed with people and report- ers. The pie contest was always the most popular event of the culinary section. So many farm stands displayed their winning ribbons for the tourists to see. And it mattered for Stillwater Marina, I thought, holding my breath, not just for me.

A woman with braided hair and an orange JUDGE tag picked up the microphone. "Once again, we had the most fabulous sampling of berry pies this year. Let's give a hand to all of our pie makers!"

After the applause died down, she spoke again. "And now our winners. In third place, to Ms. Lisa Banks, for her 'Very Blueberry Pie.'"

The winner shouted and ran up to receive her yellow ribbon.

"The last two pies were so tasty, it was hard to decide which was better, but second place goes to our longtime winner, Shelly Costa, for her 'Costa Farm Strawberry Pie'!"

"Yeah!" Tina yelled as her mom moved forward to receive her red ribbon.

Luke clapped my shoulder. "You could be next," he whispered.

I held my breath and wiped my sweaty hands on my pants. It was almost like standing on the edge of the cliff.

"And first place goes to a new entrant this year, for a fabulous 'Wild Berry Pie': June Farrell!"

I gasped. Mom and Eva both said, "What?!"

"The judges were impressed by the unusual berry combination, wild flavor, and exquisite crust."

"Wild flavor!" hooted Luke. "I knew it!"

"Go ahead and get your ribbon," Tina said.

I couldn't stop smiling. I had won! I pushed my hair

back. "Excuse me," I said, and the crowd moved aside so I could get through. It seemed like miles to the stage.

"Are you June Farrell?" the judge asked, her smile fading.

"Yes," I said.

"Did you enter the adult competition?"

I nodded, suddenly cold.

"Just a minute." She walked away to talk with the other judges on the side of the stage. They whispered, rereading my registration form. I couldn't look at the audience; I studied the edge of the stage, feeling small.

"She entered fair and square!" A voice rose from the crowd. I hoped it wasn't Eva, speaking up again. And then I stared. Mrs. Costa and the other winner, Lisa Banks, were approaching the stage.

"There isn't any age restriction on the pie competition," Ms. Banks said.

"And she won on the merit of her pie," Mrs. Costa said.

The three judges looked at one another again, and back at the rule book. They all nodded. The first judge took up the microphone again. "Then it's decided. First place goes to June Farrell!"

The noise in the hall almost knocked me over. I just stood there, grinning and grinning. I held up my blue ribbon for Mom and Eva to see.

As soon as I stepped off the stage, Luke, Tina, and my moms crowded around me.

"Why didn't you tell us?" Mom asked.

"I needed a parent signature," I said. "And you had said I couldn't enter."

"She was resourceful, MJ, you have to admit," Eva said. "We're so proud of you, June."

The judge and a reporter came up, then.

"Let me shake the hand of a champion pie maker," the judge said. "I just didn't expect someone so young."

"How old are you?" the reporter asked. "I'm with the *Free Press*, and we want to do a story on the winner."

"Twelve," I said.

"Is this what you'd expect from a kid?" the reporter asked the judge.

"It's surprising, but it clearly had winning taste."

"You can taste June's pies anytime at Stillwater Marina," Mom said. "June's been helping me since she was a little girl."

I remembered my manners then. "This is my mom, MJ Farrell." I took a deep breath. "And this is my almost stepmom, Eva Lewis."

There was no hesitation, no break in the judge's smile. I'm sure, because I was watching, waiting for a flick of disapproval. It didn't happen.

"It's a pleasure to meet both of you," she said.

"This is going to be a great story!" the reporter said.

"Um," Eva said, "I'm not sure if everything about June needs to go in the paper."

"Yes, it does," I said, remembering Ms. Flynn's words. "They're even getting married next week."

"Congratulations," the judge said as the reporter started scribbling.

Mom put her arms around me.

For the first time I began to believe that maybe there were fewer Mr. Costas in Vermont and more people like the judge and Ms. Flynn.

chapter fifteen

FOR DAYS, I woke up dreaming of blue—blue ribbon, blueberries, blue lake, blue dress. The ribbon was still on my desk where I could see it each morning. It was right next to the newspaper clipping that said "12-year-old Wins Pie Competition." Almost exactly the way I had imagined.

Blueberry season was over, but the day I had to wear my blueberry dress was nearing. The wedding. Saying out loud that I had two moms to the reporter—just matter-of-factly, that's the way it is—had felt good. And it had been easier than I thought. But I was still uneasy about the ceremony. What if something went wrong?

August third arrived, hot and muggy. *All the guests are going to want to swim,* I thought as I put on my bathing suit. I looked out the window and snapped on the weather radio. "Northwest wind today, ten to fifteen knots, water temperature sixty-six degrees."

A good swimming day. I checked Luke's signal; it was red. And I could see him rowing over. Trouble? Could he have seen another sign by the marina?

"Where are you going, June? We have to be ready by ten for the wedding!" Mom called as I ran down to the dock.

"It's important," I yelled. "I'll be right back!"

I grabbed his line, secured it, and held the edge of the boat steady. My face must have looked worried.

Luke grinned. "It's a swimming emergency. Let's go before we have to get dressed up!"

I sat down on the dock. It wasn't funny. "Red should be for real emergencies."

Luke looked at me sideways. "What's wrong?"

"Today's a big deal," I said. "What if I mess up — drop my bouquet or trip? What if Mom is marrying the wrong person?"

We splashed our feet in the water.

Making a family was hard. I remembered leaving Eva out in the canoe, and the time she and Mom had yelled in the kitchen. And I remembered her holding on to the motorboat with Luke at the helm.

"I know!" Luke jumped up.

"What?"

Luke didn't answer; he took off across the meadow and into the woods. Running behind him, I knew where he was going. And he was right; it was time. If I was going to have the courage to be the maid of honor at my mom's wedding, I had to repeat my performance at the cliff's edge.

I hadn't been back since the accident. After the fair, Mom and I had been so busy at Stillwater Marina. The article about me and my prize-winning pie — and where you could buy more like it — had been better than any plan we could have created to fight the flyer made by the Take Back Vermont people. It was like Ms. Flynn's advice: It's better to speak up so you don't miss the chance to experience other people at their best.

The mosquitoes found Luke and me soon after we entered the woods. We walked quietly, without speaking. I worried: Was I brave enough to jump again?

"Here's where the champion blueberries were," I said.

"And here's the ledge," Luke said. "I still can't believe you did it."

"I had to." I remembered again the rain, the cold, the fear.

"Ready? I'll go first."

Luke draped his shirt across a cedar branch. From the ledge, he looked up at me.

"It's easier if you think of a word that you want to yell,

something that you've always wanted to shout at the top of your lungs," Luke said.

"Like what?"

"Turkey sandwich!" he said. "Or peanut butter bananas!"

I grinned.

Luke moved to the edge. "Twisted Sister!" he hollered, and threw himself off.

I held my breath—I couldn't help it. My palms were sweaty just watching him. In a moment, he was up, splashing and shouting, "C'mon!"

"OK," I said, but I didn't feel ready. I stepped carefully down to the ledge, clinging to the side. *Come on, June,* I said to myself. *You've already done this once.* I looked across the lake then, to the hills beyond. In the distance, I saw Camel's Hump, rising above the hills. Early explorers had called the mountain something in French, something that meant resting lion. I was like that, too, brave and at peace. I had stood up to bullies, I had won a pie contest, I had saved Tim. I could jump off the cliff.

"Wild Berry Pie!" I shouted, and jumped.

My heart was in my throat; the wind dried my sweat; then I hit. Bubbles exploded around me, and I pulled to the top.

"Way to go!" Luke said as soon as I surfaced.

"I didn't get water up my nose this time!"

He laughed, and I couldn't stop grinning. My heart felt so full, like a life jacket keeping me afloat.

"Race you to the cliff!"

I swam through the deep water, just a few strokes behind Luke.

LATER, AS I brushed my hair for the wedding — scratching my new mosquito bites — I savored that flight off the cliff. Before this summer, I couldn't have done it.

I twirled around, watching my blueberry dress billow. I studied my face, the face of a cliff jumper and champion pie maker. I was ready for anything — middle school and to be maid of honor at Mom and Eva's wedding.

I ran outside to the garden. White cloth-covered tables had been set up, and on each one was a vase of Queen Anne's lace. Eva kept smoothing down edges. She looked nice in her wine-red dress and her hair glistening.

"You can stop," I said. "Everything's perfect."

Eva laughed. "You're getting to know me." She smoothed her dress. "This is probably not a good time but —"

I could tell she had something on her mind. "What?"

"There's no hurry to call me Stepmom. I'd like to earn the right to be a mom to you, June."

I glanced at the lake. The wind was picking up, and

low waves were crashing on our shore. If the lake could handle change, maybe I could.

Mom floated over like a fairy in a lilac dress. "No worries, right?"

"No worries," I said.

And it was true. Well, maybe I was nervous, but being the way we were seemed easier than hiding it.

People started arriving right on time. I was surprised by how many came — my grandma from New York, people from the hospital, and some other business owners and friends from Burlington. You could tell Eva was sad about her dad not coming, yet she smiled big when Ruth arrived in a flowery hat. Ms. Flynn gave me a hug when she walked in. And, of course, Luke was there with Joe. They looked funny in their ties.

"June." Luke pointed to the gate. Tim was walking in. I couldn't believe it. I hadn't expected any Costas, but Tim, Tina, and Mrs. Costa were here. The yard felt extra sunny.

"June!" Tim ran over for a hug. Tina waved and sat down with her mom.

When the music started, I walked down the aisle alone, with my bouquet. I took slow steps, trying not to rush, like Mom had told me. I was glad when I saw Tina grinning at me. And then I stood next to the justice of the peace and watched Eva and Mom come down the aisle side by side.

They were like a violet bloom together, all lilac and burgundy, walking with their arms linked. You'd think that two people about to get married would be trying to catch each other's eyes, but I realized they were trying to catch mine. Mom was smiling at me, like always, with love and humor, but it was Eva's serious smile that made a lump rise in my throat. *These are my parents,* I thought. *This is my family.*

The justice of the peace spoke about the bold beauty of Vermont and the commitment of my two moms to each other, and to me. Mom and Eva exchanged new rings, really pretty ones with blue stones. They reminded me of wild blueberries and the lake, too, and I bet that was what Mom was thinking. And then Mom and Eva kissed.

I looked for Luke. He was smiling at me, and suddenly I knew. I had felt it every time Luke had held my hand this summer. I turned back to my parents, holding the hope of love like a gift in my hands. And then it was over — and everyone cheered.

"Congratulations," Mrs. Costa said to Mom and Eva.

"Thank you for coming," Mom said, and I could tell she meant it.

Luke and I stood in line for cake. Luke's dad had given Mom and Eva a sculpture for the garden, and we stared at its entwining waves and circles.

"I like it a lot," I told Luke.

"Thanks," he said. "You know, my dad's not so crazy to live with after all."

"Neither is Eva."

"I guess we'll never know who put that 'Take Back Vermont' sign by the shop," he said.

"It doesn't matter," Ms. Flynn said as she came up and gave me a hug. "I was so proud of you up there."

"It was almost like I was getting married," I said.

"Here's our girl," Mom said, putting her hands on my shoulder. "Our hero."

"Saving a kid and the shop." Eva planted a kiss on me. "All in one summer."

"I just did what was right," I said.

"When did you grow up?" Mom whispered.

It felt good.

Tomorrow, I had a few things to add to my special box: Mom and Eva's wedding announcement I had cut out of the newspaper, the article about my champion pie, and my blue ribbon.

Wild Berry Pie

PIE CRUST:

13 Tbsps butter
2 cups all-purpose flour
1 tsp salt
¼ cup water

FILLING:

2 cups blueberries
1 cup strawberries, hulled and sliced
1 cup black raspberries
¾ cup sugar
⅓ cup flour
½ tsp cinnamon
juice of half a lemon
1 Tbsp butter

TO MAKE THE CRUST:

Cut butter into flour and salt until pieces are mar-
ble-size. Carefully add water, mixing until dough is
moist but not wet (when the butter warms up, the
dough gets soft). Divide into two balls. Roll one between two sheets of wax paper. Peel away one sheet
and press dough into bottom of pie plate. Leave top
wax paper on and put the second ball and pie plate in
the refrigerator while mixing the filling (you don't
want the butter in the dough getting too warm).

TO MAKE THE FILLING:

Pour all the berries in a bowl. Mix sugar, flour, and
cinnamon together in a measuring cup, then pour
over fruit. Mix gently, add the lemon juice, and mix
gently again.

Take out the pie dish, remove the wax paper, and
pour the filling into the pie crust. Dot with butter. Roll out top crust and cover the pie. Poke holes
in the top. Then, using two fingers and one thumb,
pinch a fluted edge to seal pie. Line edges with tin
foil to reduce burning, but remove the tin foil in
the last 10 minutes of baking.

Bake at 425 degrees F for 35 to 40 minutes. Pie
is ready when juice bubbles through the holes (so
don't go swimming and forget about your pie!).

I'm so grateful to the people at Vermont College of Fine Arts, a magical place for book lovers and writers. A special thank-you to the WONTONS and Poetry Farmers for nurturing creativity and laughter during the mad early-parenting years. I'm also grateful to my agent, Alison Picard, for believing in the book, and my editor, Christine Krones, for loving it. And to John Schlag—thanks for everything.